格雷的老爸

格雷的老妈

格雷的哥哥
——罗德里克

格雷的同学
——弗雷格

格雷的弟弟
——曼尼

DIARY

of a Wimpy Kid

小屁孩日记②

——谁"动"了"千年奶酪"

［美］杰夫·金尼 著

陈万如 译

格雷的"死党"
——罗利

格雷

·广州·

广东省出版集团

新世纪出版社

本书简体中文版由美国 Harry N. Abrams 公司通过中国 Creative Excellence Rights Agency 独家授权

版权合同登记号：19-2008-097 号

图书在版编目（CIP）数据

小屁孩日记②：谁"动"了"千年奶酪"／［美］杰夫·金尼著；
陈万如译. —2 版. —广州：新世纪出版社，2012.6（2013.6重印）
ISBN 978-7-5405-3914-6/04

Ⅰ．小…　Ⅱ．①杰…　②陈…　Ⅲ．日记体小说-美国-现代　Ⅳ．I712.45

中国版本图书馆 CIP 数据核字（2008）第 203531 号

出　版　人：孙泽军
选题策划：林　铨　王小斌
责任编辑：王小斌　傅　琨
责任技编：王建慧

小屁孩日记②——谁"动"了"千年奶酪"
XIAOPIHAI RIJI②——SHUI DONG LE QIANNIANNAILAO
［美］杰夫·金尼　著　陈万如　译

出版发行：新世纪出版社
　　　　　（广州市大沙头四马路10号　邮政编码：510102）
经　　销：全国新华书店
印　　刷：河源市天才印务有限公司
开　　本：890mm×1240mm　1/32
印　　张：7　　字　数：110千字
版　　次：2012年6月第2版
印　　次：2013年6月第25次印刷
印　　数：261 001～286 000
定　　价：16.80元

质量监督电话：020-83797655　购书咨询电话：020-83781545

"小屁孩之父" 杰夫·金尼致中国粉丝

中国的"哈屁族":

你们好!

从小我就对中国很着迷,现在能给中国读者写信真是我的荣幸啊。我从来没想过自己会成为作家,更没想到我的作品会流传到你们的国家,一个离我家十万八千里的地方。

当我还是个小屁孩的时候,我和我的朋友曾试着挖地洞,希望一直挖下去就能到地球另一端的中国。不一会儿,我们就放弃了这个想法(要知道,挖洞是件多辛苦的事儿啊!);但现在通过我的这些作品,我终于到中国来了——只是通过另一种方式,跟我的想象有点不一样的方式。

谢谢你们让《小屁孩日记》在中国成为畅销书。我希望你们觉得这些故事是有趣的,也希望这些故事对你们是一种激励,让你们有朝一日也成为作家和漫画家。我是幸运的,因为我的梦想就是成为一个漫画家,而现在这个梦想实现了。不管你们的梦想是什么,我都希望你们梦想成真。

我希望有朝一日能亲身到中国看看。这是个将要实现的梦想!

希望你们喜欢《小屁孩日记》的第五册(编者注:即中译本第9、10册)。再次感谢你们对这套书的喜爱!

杰夫

A Letter to Chinese Readers

Hello to all my fans in China!

I've had a fascination with China ever since I was a boy, and it's a real privilege to be writing to you now. I never could have imagined that I would become an author, and that my work would reach a place as far from my home as your own country.

When I was a kid, my friends and I tried to dig a hole in the ground, because we hoped we could reach China on the other side of the earth. We gave up after a few minutes (digging is hard!), but with these books, I'm getting to reach your country... just in a different way than I had imagined.

Thank you so much for making **Diary of a Wimpy Kid** a success in your country. I hope you find the stories funny and that they inspire you to become writers and cartoonists. I feel very fortunate to have achieved my dream to become a cartoonist, and I hope you achieve your dream, too... whatever it might be.

I hope to one day visit China. It would be a dream come true!

I hope you enjoy the fifth **Wimpy Kid** book. Thank you again for embracing my books!

Jeff

有趣的书，好玩的书

夏致

这是一个美国中学男生的日记。他为自己的瘦小个子而苦恼，老是会担心被同班的大块头欺负，会感慨"为什么分班不是按个头分而是按年龄分"。这是他心里一道小小的自卑，可是另一方面呢，他又为自己的脑瓜比别人灵光而沾沾自喜，心里嘲笑同班同学是笨蛋，老想投机取巧偷懒。

他在老妈的要求下写日记，幻想着自己成名后拿日记本应付蜂拥而至的记者；他特意在分班时装得不会念书，好让自己被分进基础班，打的主意是"尽可能降低别人对你的期望值，这样即使最后你可能几乎什么都不用干，也总能给他们带来惊喜"；他喜欢玩电子游戏，可是他爸爸常常把他赶出家去，好让他多活动一下。结果他跑到朋友家里去继续打游戏，然后在回家的路上用别人家的喷水器弄湿身子，扮成一身大汗的样子；他眼红自己的好朋友手受伤以后得到女生的百般呵护，就故意用绷带把自己的手掌缠得严严实实的装伤员，没招来女生的关注反而惹来自己不想搭理的人；不过，一山还有一山高，格雷再聪明，在家里还是敌不过哥哥罗德里克，还是被耍得团团转；而正在上幼儿园的弟弟曼尼可以"恃小卖小"，无论怎么捣蛋都有爸妈护着，让格雷无可奈何。

这个狡黠、机趣、自恋、胆小、爱出风头、喜欢懒散的男孩，一点都不符合人们心目中的那种懂事上进的好孩子形象，奇怪的是这个缺点不少的男孩子让我忍不住喜欢他。

人们总想对生活中的一切事情贴上个"好"或"坏"的标签。要是找不出它的实在可见的好处，它就一定是"坏"，是没有价值的。单纯的有趣，让我们增添几分好感和热爱，这难道不是比读书学习考试重要得多的事情吗?! 生活就像一个蜜糖罐子，我们是趴在桌子边踮高脚尖伸出手，眼巴巴地瞅着罐子的孩子。有趣不就是蜂蜜的滋味吗?

翻开这本书后，我每次笑声与下一次笑声之间停顿不超过五分钟。一是因为格雷满脑子的鬼主意和诡辩，实在让人忍俊不禁。二是因为我还能毫不费劲地明白他的想法，一下子就捕捉到格雷的逻辑好笑在哪里，然后会心一笑。

小学二年级的时候我和同班的男生打架；初一的时候放学后我在黑板上写"某某某（男生）是个大笨蛋"；初二的时候，同桌的男生起立回答老师的提问，我偷偷移开他的椅子，让他的屁股结结实实地亲吻了地面……我对初中男生的记忆少得可怜。到了高中，进了一所重点中学，大多数的男生要么是专心学习的乖男孩，要么是个性飞扬的早熟少年。除了愚人节和邻班的同学集体调换教室糊弄老师以外，男生们很少再玩恶作剧了。仿佛大家不约而同都知道，自己已经过了有资格耍小聪明，并且耍完以后别人会觉得自己可爱的年龄了。

如果你是一位超过中学年龄的大朋友，欢迎你和我在阅读时光中做一次短暂的童年之旅；如果你是格雷的同龄人，我真羡慕你们，因为你们读了这本日记之后，还可以在自己的周围发现比格雷的经历更妙趣横生的小故事，让阅读的美好体验延续到生活里。

要是给我一个机会再过一次童年，我一定会睁大自己还没有患上近视的眼睛，仔细发掘身边有趣的小事情，拿起笔记录下来。亲爱的读者，不知道当你读完这本小书后，是否也有同样的感觉?

片刻之后我转念一想，也许从现在开始，还来得及呢。作者创作这本图画日记那年是30岁，那么说来我还有9年时间呢。

一种简单的快乐

刘恺威

　　我接触《小屁孩日记》的时间其实并不长，是大约在一年多以前，我从香港飞回横店时，在机场的书店里看到了《小屁孩日记》的漫画。可能每一个人喜爱的漫画风格都不太一样，比如有人喜欢美式的、日系的、中国风的，有人注重写实感的，而我个人就比较偏向于这种线条简单的、随性的漫画，而且人物表情也都非常可爱。所以当时一下子就被封面吸引住了，再翻了翻内容，越看越觉得开心有趣，所以立刻就买下了它。

　　说实话，我并不认为《小屁孩日记》只是一本简单的儿童读物。我向别人推荐它的时候也会说，它是一本可以给大人看的漫画书，可以让整个人都感受到那种纯粹的开心。可能大家或多或少都会有这样的感受，当我们离开学校出来工作以后，渐渐的变得忙碌、和家人聚在一起的时间越来越少，也无法避免地接收到一些压力和负面情绪，对生活和社会的认知也变得更加复杂，有时候会感觉很累，心情烦躁，但如果真的自问为什么会这么累，究竟在辛苦追求着什么的时候，自己却又没有真正的答案……这并不是说我对成年后的生活有多么悲观，但像小孩子一样简单的快乐，确实离成年人越来越远了。但当我在看到《小屁孩日记》的时候，我却突然间想起了自己童年时那种纯真、简单的生活，这也是我决定买下这本漫画的原因之一。看《小屁孩日记》会让我把自己带回正轨，审核自己，检查一下自己最近的情绪、状况，还是要回到人的根本——开心。

　　我到现在也喜欢随手画一些小屁孩的画像来送给大家，这个也是最近一年来形成的习惯，因为自己大学读的是建筑，平时就喜欢随手画些东西，喜欢上小屁孩之后就开始画里面的人物，别看这个漫画线条简单，但想要用最简单的线条画出漫画里那种可爱的感觉，反而挺花功夫的。除了小屁孩这个主角之外，我最喜欢画的就是他的弟弟。弟弟是个特别爱搞鬼的小孩，而且长着一张让人特别想去捏他的脸。这兄弟俩的故事经常会让我想起我跟我妹妹的关系，我妹妹小时候也总是被我"欺负"，比如捏她的脸啊、整蛊她啊，但如果遇到了外人欺负妹妹，自己绝对是第一个站出来保护她的人。

十二月

星期三

　　唔，要是说这次演出出了什么好事情，那就是我再也不用担心那个"波波"的外号。

　　今天第五节课之后，我看到亚奇·凯利在走廊里麻烦缠身，看样子，我倒是终于可以松口气了。

星期日

　　学校的事没完没了，我连好好想一下圣诞节该怎么过都没有时间。现在离圣诞节只有十天不到。

　　事实上，唯一一件让我嗅到圣诞节气息的事情，是罗德里克将他的愿望单贴到冰箱上去。

罗德里克的愿望单

1.新鼓
2.新的小·货车
3.变小·的脑袋

每年我通常会列出一篇长长的愿望单，但今年圣诞，我想要的，就只是这个叫"古怪法师"的电子游戏。

今晚曼尼从头到尾翻遍整本圣诞购物目录，用红色的记号笔圈出他看中的东西。结果目录里面的每件玩具都被画上了圈圈。连巨型马达小汽车之类贵得要命的东西他都圈了出来。

看到他这样子，我决定插手进来，在这件事上给他一点大哥的金玉良言。

我跟他说，要是他挑的东西太费钱，最后他的圣诞礼物就只会是几件衣服。我说他应该只挑三四件价钱一般般的礼物，那他就会收到几件自己真正想要的东西。

当然咯，曼尼只是翻回目录开头，从头开始在每件东西上面再画一个圈。我猜他得碰过壁之后才能学聪明。

七岁那年，我想要的唯一一件圣诞礼物，是芭比娃娃的梦之屋。想要的原因，绝不是罗德里克所说的我喜欢女孩子的玩具。

我只是觉得拿它来给我的玩具士兵做堡垒会很威风。

那年爸妈看到我的愿望单后，为这件事吵了一大架。老爸发话说，让他给我买一个洋娃娃的屋子，没门。但老妈说，不管我想玩的是哪种玩具，"试验"一下总是好的。

信不信由你，老爸居然赢了这场嘴皮子仗。他让我重新写愿望单，挑些更"适合"男孩的玩具。

但我有一件圣诞节秘密武器。不管我想要啥，查理叔叔总会送给我。我跟他说，我想要芭比娃娃的梦之屋，他就一口答应下来了。

圣诞节那天，查理叔叔将礼物给我的时候，我却发现那并不是我向他要的那种。他准是走进玩具店之后，一手拿起他视线之内第一件有"芭比"这个词的东西。

所以，要是你哪个时候看到一张我双手捧着一个"沙滩乐芭比娃娃"的照片，现在你至少知道前因后果了。

老爸看到查理叔叔给我的礼物时，老大不高兴。他叫我要么扔掉它，要么将它捐给慈善机构。

但我还是把它留在身边。好吧，我承认我可能拿它出来玩过一两回。

那就是我两个星期后出现在急诊室的缘故。一只芭比娃娃的粉红鞋子堵住了我的鼻子。相信我，罗德里克永远不会让我忘记这件事。

星期四

今晚我和老妈出去，给教堂的"爱心树"买一份礼物。"爱心树"基本上跟秘密圣诞老人一样，你可以在那里放一份礼物，送给生活艰难的人。

老妈给我们的"爱心树"朋友挑了一件红色羊毛衣。

我费尽唇舌想说服老妈买些比这酷得多的东西，比如说电视机、雪糕机之类的。

设想一下，要是你全部的圣诞礼物只是一件羊毛衣。

我敢断定，我们的"爱心树"朋友会把他的毛衣扔进垃圾桶，一同被扔掉的还有我们在感恩节募捐食物活动中送给他的十罐红薯。

圣诞节

今早我睡醒之后走下楼，看见已经有无数件礼物堆在圣诞树下了。我开始在里面掘宝，却几乎找不到一件上面写有我的名字的。

可曼尼的收获之丰富就像刚打劫回来的强盗一样。在购物目录圈出的每样东西他都收到了，一点不假。所以我打赌，他会庆幸没听我的话。

我还是找到几件上面写着我的名字的东西，但都是些书啊袜子啊之类的。

我躲在沙发后面的角落里拆礼物，因为我不喜欢在老爸的周围打开礼物。不管什么时候有人拆礼物，老爸就会看准时机扑过来，一下就把拆出来的包装纸清理掉。

　　我送了一部玩具直升机给曼尼，送了一本写摇滚乐队的书给罗德里克。罗德里克给我的也是一本书，不用说，他没有包起来。他送我的是一本《俏妞莉儿最佳选集》。"俏妞莉儿"是报纸上最没劲的漫画。我有多讨厌它，罗德里克心知肚明。让我算算，这已经是我连续第四年从他那里得到一本"俏妞莉儿"。

　　我也送了礼物给老爸老妈。每年我都送他们一样的东西，那些东西做父母的都受用。

　　11点左右其他亲戚陆续现身，中午时分查理叔叔来了。

　　查理叔叔带着一个满载礼物的大袋子。 他从袋子最上面抽出
我的礼物。

　　盒子的包装大小·和形状跟"古怪法师"游戏一模一样，我就
知道查理叔叔会帮我达成心愿。 老妈预备好照相机之后，我撕开
礼物的包装。

但是，那只是一幅查理叔叔 8 英寸 × 10 英寸的照片。

　　估计在掩盖自己的失望这件事上，我做得太糟糕了。老妈气疯了。我只能说，幸好我还是个小孩。说这话是因为，要我像大人们一样，收到那样的礼物还喜笑颜开，我可办不到。

我走上楼去，到自己的房间休息一会儿。几分钟后老爸来敲我的门。他告诉我，他准备给我的礼物放在车库里，因为体积太大，不好包装。

我走到车库一看，一副崭新的举重器械在那里亮相。

那玩意儿一定所费不菲，我没胆量跟老爸说，上个星期摔跤课结束后，我对举重那些东西都没兴趣了。我吞下那些话，只说了一声"谢谢"。

我估摸老爸满心期待我马上俯身来几下，但我只是给自己找了个借口遁回房里去。

六点左右，亲戚们都走光了。

我坐在沙发上，眼巴巴地看着曼尼玩他的玩具，顾影自怜。这时老妈走过来，说她在钢琴后面发现一件礼物，上面写着我的名字，还写着"来自圣诞老人"。

要说那是"古怪法师"游戏带，老妈手上的盒子也太大了吧，不过去年老妈送我电子游戏机记忆卡时，就跟我耍过同样的"大盒子"花招。

于是我拆开包装，抽出礼物。这也不是"古怪法师"，是一件巨大的红色羊毛衣。

起初我以为老妈跟我玩恶作剧，因为这件毛衣和我们买给"爱心树"朋友的那件一个样。

但老妈也一脸迷惑。她说她是给我买了一盒电子游戏的呀。她闹不明白毛衣怎么会在我的盒子里。

这时我明白过来了。我跟老妈说一定是出了点岔儿，我拿了"爱心树"朋友的礼物，他拿了我的。

老妈说两份礼物她用了一模一样的包装纸，一定是她在标签上写名字的时候搞混了。

但老妈说，这样真好。那个"爱心树"朋友收到这么一件礼物准会高兴得不得了。

我只好解释说，你得有一部游戏机和一台电视机才能玩"古怪法师"。这盒游戏带子对那人毫无用处。

尽管我的圣诞节过得不怎么样，但我敢肯定那个"爱心树"朋友过得比我还没劲十倍。

我对今年圣诞节不抱希望了，便到罗利家去。

我忘了给罗利买礼物，所以就在罗德里克送我的《俏妞莉儿最佳选集》上打了个蝴蝶结。

这招看起来还挺管用呢。

罗利爸妈腰缠万贯，我总可以指望在他们那里收到一份大礼。

　　但罗利说今年他亲自为我挑选礼物。 说着他带我到屋外看礼物。

　　罗利这么大肆炒作他的礼物，我以为他准是买了宽屏电视机或者摩托车。

　　又一次，我让自己的期望值飙得太高了。

　　罗利给我买了一辆"大轮子"。 要是时光倒流到小·学三年级的时候，我估计自己会觉得这礼物帅呆了。 可我不晓得现在该拿一辆"大轮子"怎么办。

　　罗利对"大轮子"的兴致高得不得了，我只好卖力地露出快活的样子。

嘻，多谢啦

我们走回屋里，罗利让我看他圣诞节的战利品。

不用说，他的收获比我丰富得多。他连"古怪法师"都有，那我至少能在他家玩上这个游戏。我说的是在罗利他爸发现这个游戏有多暴力之前。

你大概永远不会想到会有人拿着《俏妞莉儿最佳选集》乐得像罗利那样。他妈说那是唯一一件他列在愿望单上却没有收到的礼物。

好了，我很高兴今天终于有人如愿以偿，收到自己想要的礼物。

新年前夜

要是你纳闷新年前夕我晚上 9 点就呆在自己房里干吗，就听我仔细道来。

今天早些时候，我和曼尼在地下室打打闹闹。地毯上有一个黑色小·线团，还拖着线头。我唬曼尼说那是蜘蛛。

接着我拈起线头在曼尼眼睛前面荡来荡去，装作要逼他吃掉。

我正准备放过曼尼，他"啪"的一声打到我的手。我的手一松，然后你猜怎么样？那笨蛋把线团吞下去了。

这下好了，曼尼完全疯掉了。他跑上楼去找老妈，我知道麻烦大了。

曼尼向老妈控诉我逼他吞蜘蛛。 我跟她说，那不是蜘蛛，只是一个小线团，拖着一根线。

老妈把曼尼带去厨房的桌子旁边。 她在桌上放了一颗种子、一颗葡萄干和一颗葡萄，让曼尼说他吞下的东西和哪一样的大小最接近。

曼尼定睛看着碟子好一阵子。

然后他走去冰箱那里，拿出一个橙子。

这就是为什么我晚上 7 点就被撵去睡觉，没机会下楼看年夜的电视特别节目。

这也是为什么我唯一的新年决心是以后再也不和曼尼玩。

一 月

星期三

我想到一个用罗利送我的"大轮子"来找乐子的办法了。玩法是这样的：一个人从山坡上骑车下来，另一个人千方百计用球砸中对方，让他从车上摔下来。

罗利做下山的第一人，我做投球手。

要击中移动目标的难度比我想象中大得多。再说我也没有怎么练习。每次罗利冲下山以后，得花十分钟推车上坡。

罗利不断吵着投球手要换人，让我来做骑手。 我可不笨。那□意儿时速 35 英里，而且没有刹车踏板。

不管怎样，今天我一次也没有砸中罗利。 但我总得找点活儿干，打发掉假期的尾巴。

星期四

我又准备去罗利家玩"大轮子"了。 但老妈下令，没把所有感谢卡写完，我哪也别想去。

我本来以为不用半小·时就能完工，但到拿起笔的时候，却发现我的大脑一片空白。

我跟你说，为你自己不想要的东西写感谢卡，一点都不容易。

我先从衣服以外的东西入手。因为我觉得感谢别人送你衣服最容易。但写了两三张之后，我意识到实际上我每张卡写的话都差不多。

亲爱的 莉迪亚阿姨：

　　真谢谢你呀，送了那么棒的 百科全书 给我！

　　你怎么知道我想要它做圣诞礼物呢？

　　我好喜欢 百科全书 放在我 书架 上的样子啊！

　　我的朋友都会羡慕我能拥有自己的 百科全书。

　　谢谢你让今年圣诞节成为我过得最好的圣诞节！

　　　　　　　　　　　　　　　　真心真意的 格雷

对刚开始的几件礼物，我的系统相当管用，但往后就不怎么样了。

亲爱的 洛蕾塔阿姨：

　　真谢谢你呀，送了那么棒的 裤子 给我！

　　你怎么知道我想要它做圣诞礼物呢？

　　我好喜欢 裤子 放在我 腿 上的样子啊！

　　我的朋友都会羡慕我能拥有自己的 裤子。

　　谢谢你让今年圣诞节成为我过得最好的圣诞节！

　　　　　　　　　　　　　　真心真意的 格雷

星期五

　　今天我终于砸中罗利，让他从"大轮子"上摔下来了。但这事并不是按我预想中的方式发生的。我想用球砸他的肩膀，但没扔中。球滚到前轮下。

罗利伸开双手，想减缓摔下来的力量，但他的身子还是重重地压在左手上。我以为他会跟没事一样，马上自己坐回车上，但他没有。

我使出浑身解数哄他高兴，但平时让他笑得合不拢嘴的段子没一个管用。

于是我知道他一定摔得很惨。

星期一

圣诞假期完了。我们回到学校。你还记得罗利的"大轮子"事故吧？噢，他的手骨折了。现在他得挂着石膏绷带。今天每个人都围着他，好像他是个英雄或是什么大人物似的。

我尝试从罗利急升的人气中分一杯羹，谁知好处没捞到，还惹火烧身。

午饭时，好几个女生邀请罗利到她们的桌子坐，好让她们喂他吃饭。

让我真正不忿的是，罗利是右撇子，骨折的是他的左手。 他自己吃饭一点问题没有。

星期二

我意识到罗利的伤是个极好的幌子。 我决定是时候亲自负伤一次了。

我从家里拿了一些纱布，把我的手裹得跟真的受伤了一样。

我搞不懂为什么那帮女生没有像围着罗利团团转那样围着我。但没多久我就明白问题出在哪了。

瞧，打石膏挂绷带是多好的招数，因为人人都想在上面签个名。但要用钢笔在纱布上签名就困难多了。

于是我想了一个解决办法，自我感觉这法子不比打石膏差。

这个主意也一败涂地。我的纱布确实也吸引了几个人来看，但放心，那些人不是我看得上的那一类。

星期一

　　上星期开始是这学年的第三个学段。 我的课全是以前没上过的。 我选上的其中一门叫"自主学习"。

　　我想选的是"高级家政"啊。 我"初级家政"的成绩那么好。

　　不过，针线活做得好并不能让你在学校更受欢迎。

说回正题，"自主学习"这个东西在我们学校还是第一次试验。

课程内容是老师给全班学生布置一个作业项目，往后老师整个学期都不来教室，你得和其他人一起完成这个作业。

问题是，你做好了作业，其他每个人都会得到同样的分数。我发现瑞奇·费舍尔也在我这个班。这真是个大问题。

瑞奇蜚声全校的名言是，谁给他 50 美分，他就捡起书桌脚下粘着的口香糖，放在嘴里嚼一番。所以我对我们的期末成绩，真的不抱多大期望了。

星期二

今天我们知道"自主学习"任务了。猜猜那是啥？我们要做一个机器人。

起初每个人都有点抓狂，因为我们以为得一切从零开始。

好在达奈尔先生跟我们讲，不用真的造一个机器人出来。我们只需要设计好我们的机器人长什么样，还有就是它能做什么事情。

说完他就离开教室。全靠我们自己了。我们马上开动脑筋想点子。我在黑板上写了几个。

这个机器人可以
替我做作业
洗碟子
替我煮早餐
替我刷牙

　　每个人都对我的想法赞叹不已。 其实嘛，这个想法来得非常简单。 我就是写下所有我讨厌做的事情。

　　有几个女生走到教室前面，她们自有主张。 她们擦掉我写的，写上她们自己的计划。

　　她们要发明一种机器人，不但给你提供约会的建议，还有不同颜色的唇膏附在十个指头上。

　　我们男生一致认为，这是我们听过的最傻气的想法。 结果我们分成女生和男生两组。 男生去了教室的另一头。 女生就站在黑板旁边讨论。

　　认真干事的人已经聚在一起，我们开工了。 有人出了个点子：你对机器人说出你的名字，它就会做出反馈。

嗨，鲍勃。真高兴
见到你呀，鲍勃。

　　这时有人提出，你的名字里不能带脏字，因为机器人不应该骂人。于是我们决定要列一张清单，把机器人不应该说的所有字眼都写在上面。

　　我们想尽所有常用的脏字，但瑞奇·费舍尔说了二十多个我们从来没有听说过的脏字。

　　就这样瑞奇成为对这个作业贡献最多的人。

　　就在下课铃响之前，达奈尔先生回到教室，检查我们的进度。他拿起我们正在上面写字的纸，大声读了出来。

　　长话短说，这一年余下的"自主学习"课程被取消了。

好吧，至少是对我们男生取消了。要是将来的机器人手指头沾着樱桃味的唇膏到处走，现在你该知道它从哪里冒出来的吧。

星期四

今天学校召集了一次全体大会，放映一部名叫《做自己真棒》的电影。这电影年年都放。

电影尽是说你应该为自己现在的样子感到高兴，不要改变自己的任何东西。

老实对你说，我认为这种说给孩子听的话真是愚蠢透顶，尤其是对我们学校那些家伙说。

晚些时候，学校宣布，交通安全队有几个空缺的位子。我的脑筋开始转起来。

要是有人找巡逻员的碴儿，他们就会被停课。没错，我能把我得到的任何特殊保护都用上。

再说，呆在一个有权力的位置，也许对我有好处。

我走下楼去文思基先生的办公室报名做巡逻队员。我说服了罗利，他也报名了。本来以为文思基先生会叫我们做几个引体向上或者立定跳远，好证明我们能胜任这份工作。没想到他当场就把束带和徽章给了我们。

文思基先生说这个职位专为一个特别任务而设。和我们学校一墙之隔有一所小学。他们设有一个半日制的幼儿班。

文思基先生要我们中午时护送上午班的学生走回家。我知道这就是说头 20 分钟的代数课我们上不成了。

罗利一定也明白过来，因为他开口说话了。还没等他说完第一句话，我在桌子下面邪恶地掐了他一把。

可是我们就上
不成——哎哟！

我简直不敢相信自己的好运。我就要拿到"紧急欺凌保护"和免上半节代数课的通行证，而我连一根指头都不需要动。

星期二

今天是我们上任交通安全员的第一天。我和罗利不像其他巡逻队员那样要站岗，那就是说，上学时间前的一个小时我们不用站在外面冻成冰棍。

站岗没我们的份，但点名时间前餐厅免费提供给其他安全队员的热巧克力，我们的一份可就不能少啰。

我捡到的另一个大便宜是，第一节课可以迟到十分钟。

我跟你说，补上安全队员这个肥缺我赚大了。

到了 12:15，我和罗利走出学校，护送幼儿园小·孩回家。这段路得走 45 分钟，等我们回到学校，还有 20 分钟就下代数课了。

护送小·孩回家毫不费事，不过有个小·孩身上的味道慢慢有点不对头。我觉得他可能在裤子里出了点事故。

他千方百计要通知我这件事，不过我只是直视前方，一步不停。我会把这些孩子带回家，但你放心，我可没有揽上跟尿布沾边的活儿。

二　月

星期三

　　今天下了这个冬天的第一场雪。学校停课了，本来数学课我们要测验。自从我做了交通安全员，就有点懒洋洋。所以停课了我非常兴奋。

　　我打电话给罗利，叫他来我家。过去这几年，我和他一直在说着要堆出世界上最大的雪人。

我说"世界上最大的雪人"的时候，可不是说笑的。我们的目标是进入"吉尼斯世界纪录大全"。

咔嚓

不过，每次我们认真起来要为世界纪录奋斗的时候，雪已经融了，我们的一线希望就成为泡影。今年我可要马上动手。

罗利一到，我们便开始滚第一个雪球，做底下的大球。我琢磨了一下，要想打破世界纪录，雪球至少得有八英尺高。但这雪球真的很重，我们滚几步就得歇一歇，好喘上几口气。

呼哧！嘿咻！

我们歇脚时，老妈出来准备去市场买菜。但大雪球挡住车子的去路。于是我们在她身上赚了一些免费劳动力。

歇够了，我和罗利一直往前推着雪球走，走到我们走不动为止。回头一看，我们搞出来的乱子尽收眼底。

雪球太重了，老爸秋天刚铺的草皮全粘在上面。

我本来巴望着天再下几英寸的雪，盖住这些痕迹，但跟以前一样，在这时雪停了。

要堆世界上第一大雪人的计划破产了，于是我想出一个更妙的主意，让这个雪球物尽其用。

　　每回下雪，威利大街的小孩就跑到我们的小山坡上滑雪橇，全然不管这里并不是他们的地盘这一事实。

　　明儿一早，等威利大街的小屁孩们爬上我们的坡时，我和罗利就会给他们上一课。

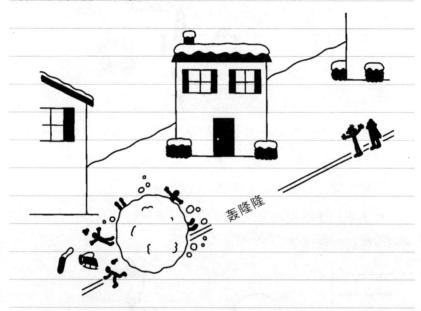

轰隆隆

星期四

　　今早我一觉醒来，雪已经开始化了。我立马让罗利赶来我家。

　　等罗利现身的空当，我看到曼尼用我们滚雪球掉下的边角余料堆雪人，费的那个劲呀。

　　真有点可怜见的。

　　我真的控制不住自己不去做接下来的这件事。倒霉的是，就在我作案之际，老爸刚好站在房子前面的窗前。

　　本来老爸已经对我扯掉草皮的事怀恨在心，我知道自己在劫难逃。我听到车库门打开的声音，老爸走出来了。他扛着铲子，气冲冲往外走。三十六计，走为上计。

但老爸是冲着我的雪球而来，不是我。不到一分钟光景，他一笔勾销了我们的艰苦劳动。

几分钟后罗利来了。我觉得刚才发生的事会让他很激动。

我想他一心要把雪球滚下山坡，所以他非常生气。但注意了：罗利因为我爸干的事而对我很生气。

我跟罗利说我爸是个大小孩，我们进行了一次铲雪比赛。眼看我们就要来一场全武打的时候，我们遭到从大街上来的伏击。

原来是威利大街的小孩在玩"打了就跑"。

要是我的语文老师列文太太在现场，我敢保证她会说："这场面正好配得上'反讽'这个词。"

星期三

今天学校宣布，校报漫画撰稿人之位招贤。报纸上只有一栏漫画，在此之前一直被一个叫布莱恩·利特尔的小·屁孩霸占着。

布莱恩的漫画叫"古怪狗"，在报纸上刚露面的时候，确实令人忍俊不禁。

但最近一段时间，布莱恩一直用漫画栏目处理私事。我猜这就是校报裁掉他的原因。

嘿,古怪狗,说点趣事吧!

其实今天我在思考一些严肃的问题。

苏珊·林姆,布莱恩很抱歉他在储物柜后面吻了你最好的朋友蕾切尔。要是你看到这期漫画,希望你能明白他的心意,并且从心底里原谅他。

还有一件事:巴利·帕玛,你还欠布莱恩五美元没还你这懒鬼!

　　一听到这个消息,我就知道我得试一试。 "古怪狗"让布莱恩·利特尔蜚声校园,我也想这样出名一把。

　　在学校里出名的滋味我尝过一次。 那次我在学校的反吸烟海报比赛中获得 "荣誉提名奖"。

　　我不过是拿纸蒙了罗德里克的重金属摇滚杂志上的一幅插图。 好在没人发现这一点。

别抽烟,不然你就会像我一样。

得了第一名的小屁孩叫克里斯·卡尼，让我不忿的是，克里斯每天至少抽掉一包烟。

星期四

我和罗利决定组队，一起画一套漫画。放学后他来我家，我们就开工了。

我们很快信笔画出几个人物，后来证明这一步是最容易的。为了想出几个段子我们绞尽脑汁，有点撞上墙壁的感觉。

① 原文"Don't Smoke. Lt's a Joke."可有两种解读。一是"叫你别吸烟是跟你开玩笑的"；一是"吸烟是拿生命开玩笑"。显然校方采用第二种解读，所以克里斯会得奖，但实际上他是用第一种解读。

最后我终于想到一条妙计。我想出了一个漫画系列，每组最后一格的趣语都是"祖维妈妈①"。

那样子，我们就不会因为想不出笑话而卡住，可以集中精力在图画上。

前几组漫画，我又写底本又画人物，罗利负责图画外面的方框。

踩到地上的缝隙，你妈就要断背脊②

好，踩中了!

嗨，提米，你妈妈被香蕉皮滑倒了，还有，她死了。

祖维妈妈!

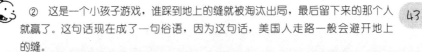

① 这里是音译，这句话本身无义，只是念出来好玩。

② 这是一个小孩子游戏，谁踩到地上的缝就被淘汰出局，最后留下来的那个人就赢了。这句话现在成了一句俗语，因为这句话，美国人走路一般会避开地上的缝。

罗利开始抱怨自己没事可干，于是我让他写了几组底本。

但跟你实话实说吧，文字活被罗利接过去后，漫画的质量明显掉了下来。

到最后，我对"祖维妈妈"腻歪了，就让罗利接过大部分的活。

信不信由你，罗利的画工比他的文笔还要糟糕。

　　我告诉罗利，也许我们该来几个新点子，可他只想继续"祖维妈妈"。画完以后，他打包好自己的大作，回家了。对我来说这也许是好事。我可真的不想跟一个画人不画鼻子的小·屁孩共事。

星期五

　　昨天罗利离开后，我确实好好画了几组漫画。我创作的人物叫呆子克雷登，我画得轻车熟路。

呆子克雷登　　作者格雷·赫夫利

嗨，我叫克雷登。

错了，你的名字是"斯图亚特·彼德"。

噢。嗨，我是"斯图·彼德"①。

哈哈哈哈！

?

① "斯图·彼德"发音跟英语单词"愚蠢的"一样，这里克雷登被耍了一把。

我已经画了二十组，轻松得滴汗不流。

　　这个"呆子克雷登"的最大好处，就在于我永远不会为新素材不够而发愁，学校里笨蛋满街走。

　　今天我一到学校，就把我的大作交到以拉先生的办公室。他是负责校报运营的老师。不过交画的时候，我看到那里已经有一摞其他小屁孩的漫画，他们也想揽这活。

大部分作品相当不济，我也不怎么担心竞争问题。

女孩最厉害！

作者塔宾莎·卡特
丽莎·罗素

哈哈哈哈哈哈
哈哈哈！

女孩最厉害！

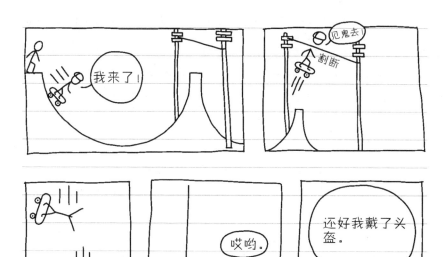

其中一个作品叫《蠢老师》，是一个叫比尔·特瑞特的小·屁孩画的。

比尔总是被罚留堂，我估计他和每个老师都有一笔账要算，这其中准有以拉先生。

所以我也不太担心比尔的漫画会入选。

在箱子里还是有一两个像样的作品。 不过，我把它们偷偷塞进以拉先生桌上的一堆文件中。

希望在我上高中之前，这些漫画不会重现人间。

星期二

今天我在早晨广播中听到自己期待的消息。

校报新一任漫画撰稿人是——格雷·赫夫利

今天午饭时段，报纸出版了，人人都在读。

我真想拿起一份报纸欣赏一下印在上面的我的名字。 但我决定还是装着若无其事一会儿。

　　我坐在餐桌一端，好腾出足够的地方给我的新崇拜者签名。可没一个人走过来夸我说我的漫画多么了不起。我隐约觉得有点不对劲。

　　我抓起一份报纸，潜入洗手间看个清楚。一看到我的漫画，我几乎气得要发心脏病。

　　以拉先生跟我说，他给我的漫画做了些"小·修·小·改"。我以为他只是说更正了拼写错误之类。哪知他是挥起屠刀。

　　他毁掉的这组是我的得意之作之一，我原来的版本中，呆子克雷登在考数学，他不小心把试卷吃进肚子里；人笨成这样，老师也忍不住朝他嚷嚷。

　　到以拉先生动完手脚以后，你压根认不出它的原来面目。

好学的克雷登　　　　　　　　　　作者:格雷·赫夫利

谢谢。孩子们，如果你希望学到更多数学知识，一定要在汉弗莱先生的办公时间找他谈谈哦。或者到图书馆，去看看数学和科学类新近上架的书本！

所以我相当肯定，一定时间内我都不需要给别人签名。

三 月

今天，正当我和罗利在餐厅里和其他交通安全员一道享受着热巧克力时，广播响起来了。

罗利·杰弗逊，立即到文思基先生的办公室报告。

罗利下楼到文思基先生的办公室去。十五分钟后罗利回来了，看样子他受打击了，有点发愣。

事情很明显，文思基先生收到一个家长的来电，说他们亲眼看到，罗利护送幼儿园小·孩回家的时候，"恐吓"了他们。这让文思基先生气疯了。

罗利说文思基先生朝他叫嚷了快十分钟，说他的行为"让徽章蒙羞"。

　　我觉得我也许知道这到底是怎么一回事。上星期，第四节课罗利要测验，所以我一个人送小孩回家。

　　那天早上下雨了，人行道上的虫子非常多。于是我打定主意要逗这些小孩玩一玩。

咿——！！！

　　不巧住在那里的一位女士看到我的一举一动，她站在她家前门朝我叫嚷。

　　那是欧文太太，她和罗利的妈妈很熟络。她准是以为我是罗利，因为那时我借了罗利的外套穿。而且我也没打算要改正她的错误。

　　要不是今天罗利挨骂，我压根不记得还有这回事了。

　　说回刚才的事，文思基先生要罗利明天早上向那些幼儿园小孩道歉，罗利还得接受一个星期的停职处罚。

　　我知道我应该向文思基先生坦白，挑着虫子追小孩跑的人是我。但我现在暂时没准备去纠正这个冤案。我知道要是我去自首，热巧克力的优待就没了。这个甜头足以让我暂时保持沉默。

　　晚饭时，妈妈看得出来我有些心事。饭后她到我的房间里找我聊天。

　　我告诉她自己处境艰难，不知道该怎么办。

　　在这件事情上，我要大大称赞老妈一番。她没有刺探我，也没有套出全部的细节。她只说了一句，我应该努力去做"正确的事情"，因为正是我们的选择决定了我们会成为怎样的人。

　　我明白这是一个正当的忠告。但我仍然没有百分之百地肯定明天要怎么做。

星期四

　　唉，我整夜辗转反侧，想着罗利的事。最后我终于打定主意。正确的选择就是这次让罗利舍己为人。

小朋友，很抱歉我吓唬了你们。

　　放学回家的路上，我跟罗利坦白了，告诉他事情的真相，我才是挑着虫子追小孩跑的罪魁祸首。

　　然后我跟他说，我们俩从这件事都可以学聪明。我说我学到了以后在欧文太太房子前面做事得小心点，他也上了宝贵的一课，那就是：留心你把外套借给谁了。

老实跟你说，我的信息似乎没有传到罗利那里。

我们本来约好今天放学后到外面玩，但罗利说他只想回家打个盹。

我真的不能怪他。要是今天早上我没有喝热巧克力，我也会无精打采。

我一到家，就看到老妈在门里等我。

老妈带我出去，特别赏了我一个冰琪淋。 这一整段小·插曲教会我的是，偶尔听一下妈妈的话，也不是件坏事。

星期二

今天广播又有一个公告，老实对你说，它的到来我早已料到几分。

我知道自己被捕归案只是一个时间问题。

我走进文思基先生的办公室时，看见他气得七窍生烟。 文思基先生跟我说一个"匿名线人"向他告发，我才是那个虫子事件的真凶。

接着他通知我，我被解除了交通安全员的职务，这个决定"立即生效"。

好吧，不用请侦探来查都知道，那个匿名线人就是罗利。

我简直不敢相信罗利会那样子在背后捅我一刀。我坐在办公室被文思基先生狠狠教训的时候，我一直在想，我要记着跟我的朋友上一课"什么是忠诚"。

今天的晚些时候，罗利恢复了安全员的职务。请注意：他居然升职了。文思基先生说罗利"在错误的怀疑下展示出尊严"。

罗利这样打我小报告，我本来盘算着要让他尝点苦头，但之后我意识到一些事情。

六月份的时候，全体交通安全队员会到"六面旗"①旅行，他们可以带一个朋友同行。我要保证罗利知道我就是他的那个人。

星期二

就像我之前说的，被踢出交通安全队最糟糕的后果是没了热巧克力的特殊待遇。

每天早上，我去餐厅的后门，好让罗利接应我。不过，要么是我的朋友耳朵聋了，要么是他在拍交通安全队其他小头目的马屁忙不过来，否则他不可能注意不到门窗后的我。

  ① "六面旗"是美国连锁主题乐园，园内有各种刺激的游乐设施。

我仔细一想，其实罗利最近一直对我完全不理不睬。 那真丢脸，因为如果我没记错，他正是那个出卖我的人。

尽管最近一段时间罗利完全是个混蛋，我还是想尽办法打破僵局。 但那也不管用了。

四 月

<u>星期五</u>

自从虫子事件之后，罗利放学后都是和柯林·李一起玩。 让我不爽的是柯林本来应该是我的备用朋友。

那两个人的表现非常可笑。 今天，罗利和柯林穿上一样的衣服，让我简直想吐。

今天晚饭过后，我看见罗利和柯林一起走上小山坡，一副哥们的样子。

柯林拿着自己的睡袋，于是我知道今晚他要在罗利家留宿。

我想了一下，好吧，两个人才能唱一场对台戏。回击罗利最好的办法是给自己找一个新朋友。可背运的是，那时候我能想起来的唯一一个人是弗雷格。

我带着自己的睡袋往弗雷格家走，好让罗利看到在朋友方面我也有另外一个选项。

到了目的地，我看见弗雷格站在他家的前院，拿着一根木棍戳风筝。这个时候我开始觉得，搭上弗雷格也许不是最好的办法。

气喘吁吁

罗利也在他家前院站着，盯着我看。所以我知道自己没有退路了。

我自己登门走进弗雷格家。他妈妈说看到弗雷格有个"玩伴"她非常激动。这个词我不太热衷。

　　我和弗雷格上楼到他的房间去。 弗雷格想让我陪他玩 "古怪法师"，我保证自己会始终和他保持十英尺的距离。

　　我想好了，我应该马上给这个愚蠢的主意拉闸，回家。 但每次我朝窗外望，都看到罗利和柯林还呆在罗利家的前院。

　　我不想在那两个家伙回屋之前离开弗雷格家。 不妙的是，弗雷格让事情很快变得不受控制。 我往窗外看的时候，弗雷格翻开我的背包，吃了我放在书包里的一整包软糖。

　　弗雷格是那种一点糖果也不该吃的孩子。 两分钟之后，他就在撞墙。

弗雷格彻头彻尾像个疯子，在楼上追着我到处跑。

我不住地想，他很快就会从糖果狂热中平静下来，可他没有。最后，我把自己锁在他的洗手间里，等他走开。

11:30 左右，走廊外面安静下来。这时候弗雷格从门底塞进一张纸。

我拿起来看。

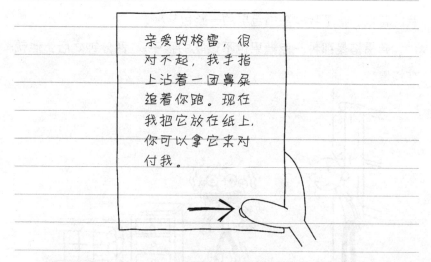

亲爱的格雷，很对不起，我手指上沾着一团鼻屎追着你跑。现在我把它放在纸上，你可以拿它来对付我。

这是我晕过去之前记得的最后一件事。

几个小时后，我恢复意识了。我一醒过来，就啪的一声开门。 听到弗雷格的房间里传出一阵鼾声，我决定三十六计，走为上计。

我让老妈老爸凌晨两点下床给我开门，他们老大不高兴。 但到了这个地步，我都不在乎这些了。

星期一

好了，我和罗利正式成为"前朋友"已经有一个月。 实话实说吧，他不在，我的日子过得更自在。

我可以想做什么就做什么，不用操心要带着那个该死的大块头。

最近放学之后，我都在罗德里克的房里混，翻遍他的东西。前几天，我找到他中学时候的一本学年手册。

手册里有每个学生的照片，罗德里克在每张照片上面都写了评语，所以你可以知道他对同年级的每个人感觉如何。

偶尔我会在城里遇见罗德里克的老同学。我要记得感谢罗德里克，因为他让去教堂做礼拜这件事变得趣味十足。

不过，在罗德里克的学年手册里，最有意思的是"班级之星"那一页。

放在这一页的照片是那些被选为"人气之星"和"才华之星"之类的小屁孩。

罗德里克也在"班级之星"这一页写了评语。

这个"班级之星"的玩意，确实让我的脑筋动起来。

如果你通过了投票进入"班级之星"那一页，那就意味着你可以留名青史。即便你后来名不副实也没有关系，因为印在手册上的东西变不了。

人们依然把比尔·沃森当成什么特别人物似的，尽管他最终从高中退学了。

我们偶尔仍然会在食品超市里遇到他。

我在考虑的是：这个学年过得有点失败，不过要是我能入选"班级之星"，那就可以善终了。

　　我想啊想，看哪一方面我有机会。"人气之星"和"健美之星"绝对没我份，我得找些我做到的可能性更大的东西。

　　起初我计划，也许这年余下的时间我应该穿着特别光鲜的衣服，那我就可以得到"最佳着装奖"。

　　但那样子的话，我就得和那个穿得跟圣徒一样的珍娜·斯图亚特一起拍照。

星期三

　　昨晚我躺在床上，突然灵光一闪：我应该争取做"班级活宝"。

　　要我凭风趣逗笑在学校出名不大可能，不过如果我能在投票遴选之前炮制一场好戏，那就搞定了。

图钉

五　月

星期四

　　今天上历史课时，我正费尽心思琢磨，怎么才能神不知鬼不觉放一颗图钉在沃斯先生的椅子上，但他突然说了些话，让我重新考虑我的计划。

　　沃斯先生跟我们讲，明天他约了牙医，所以会由别的老师代课。代课老师就像经典笑话，你可以说你想说的任何东西，还不会有任何麻烦。

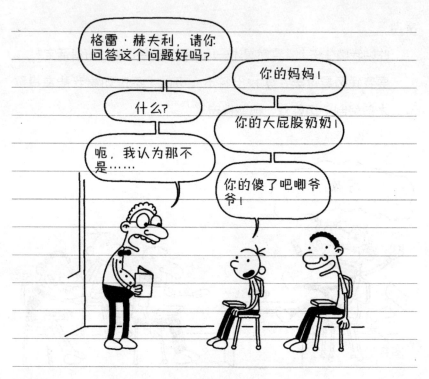

星期五

今天我走进历史课的教室，准备实施我的计划。可到了教室门口一看，你猜代课老师是谁？

世界上有那么多人可以做我们的代课老师，怎么偏偏是老妈呢。我还以为老妈参与我们学校事务的日子早已完了。

　　以前她是协助课堂事务管理的家长之一。不过在我三年级那年，老妈给我们做了一回野外公园考察的义务陪护员之后，事情发生了彻底的变化。

　　老妈准备了丰富的材料，打算引导我们这些小孩欣赏不同的动物。可我们每个人都只想看那些动物上厕所。

　　不管怎样，老妈彻底挫败了我夺取"班级活宝"称号的计划。幸好没有"最粘妈妈的儿子"这一项，不然过了今天，我会以压倒性的票数当选。

星期三

　　今天又是校报出版的日子。上回《好学的克雷登》面世之后，我就辞掉校报漫画撰稿人的差事。我一点也不在乎他们挑谁来代替我。

　　没想到午饭的时候，每个人读到漫画版都哈哈大笑。我拿起一份，看看什么东西那么好笑。翻开报纸一看，我简直不敢相信自己的眼睛。

　　那是"祖维妈妈"。当然啰，罗利的漫画以拉先生一个字也没有改。

祖维妈妈　　　　　　　　　　　　　　作者：罗利·杰弗逊

　　所以罗利把本来属于我的名气全赚走了。

连那些老师也向罗利献殷勤。 上历史课时沃斯先生不小心把粉笔掉在地上，接着他说了一句话，让我几乎吃不下午饭——

星期一

"祖维妈妈"这事真的把我气到了。 罗利得了全部美誉，可漫画是我们一起捣鼓出来的呀。 他至少可以把我的名字署为共同作者放在漫画上。

于是放学后，我去找罗利，告诉他什么是他应该说的。 但罗利说"祖维妈妈"全是他的主意，跟我没有任何关系。

我们说话的声音一定很大，因为在接下来很短的时间内，我们吸引了一群人围观。

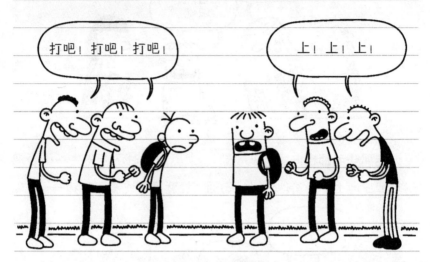

我们学校的小·屁孩每时每刻都盼着看人打架。 我和罗利试图走开，但那些家伙没看到我们甩出几拳是不会让我们脱身的。

以前我从没真正打过一场架，所以打架时要怎么站，怎么握拳，我完全没有概念。 你可以看得出，罗利也不知道自己接下来该干吗，因为他跳了起来，动作夸张得就像一只小·矮妖①。

 ① 爱尔兰民间传说中一身绿装的小妖精，顽皮淘气，人们相信捉到他们就能找到古时候财宝埋藏的地方。

我十分肯定我有能耐和罗利打上一架，但让我紧张的是罗利学过空手道。我不清楚罗利的空手道课教了什么装模作样的把戏，总之我绝对不能让罗利当场把我打趴在地上。

　　我和罗利正要动手，这时学校停车场传来一阵尖利的刹车声。一辆大卡车停了下来，从车门里挤出几个大孩子。

　　我正庆幸别人都把放在我和罗利身上的注意力转移到他们身上。可那帮大孩子往我们这边走的时候，其他小屁孩一个个溜之大吉。

　　这时候我感觉到，这几个大孩子的脸孔看起来异常熟悉。

　　我突然想起来了。他们就是万圣节晚上追着我和罗利到处跑的那帮人。他们始终是追上我们了。

　　我们还没来得及逃跑，双手就被反扣在背后。

　　那帮家伙要教训教训我们，以报万圣节当晚被我们奚落的一箭之仇。他们为怎么处置我们吵了起来。

　　不过老实跟你说，我更担心的是另外一件事。"千年奶酪"离我们站的地方只有几英尺远。它看上去比以往更让人恶心。

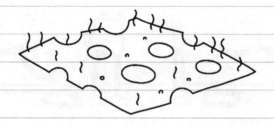

　　对着我的大孩子准是逮到我的眼神，因为紧接着，他也盯着"千年奶酪"看。我想他已经找到对付我们的办法了。

　　罗利首先被带出去。抓住他的大孩子拖着他到"千年奶酪"跟前。

　　现在，我不想说接下来到底发生了什么事。万一罗利以后想竞选总统，被人查出这些家伙逼他做的事，他可以死心了。

　　所以我只想告诉你：他们逼罗利____了"千年奶酪"。

　　我知道他们也会逼我这样做。 我慌得六神无主，因为我知道
凭我自己绝无可能冲出重围。

　　于是我花言巧语了一番。

信不信由你，这招居然管用。

　　我估计那帮大孩子出了口气心满意足，因为他们逼罗利处理完余下的"千年奶酪"后，就放我们走了。他们回到卡车上，扬长而去。

　　我和罗利一起走回家。但一路上谁也没有吭声。

　　我考虑过要不要给罗利提一下，刚才他其实可以当场耍几下空手道的招式。不过有些东西告诫我，这个想法暂时得忍住。

<u>星期二</u>

今天午饭后，老师让我们到教室外面去。

过了五秒钟，才有人反应过来：沥青地上的"千年奶酪"不翼而飞。

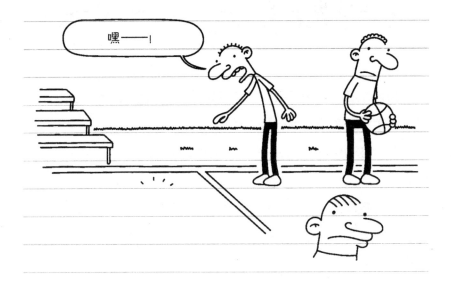

大家挤在一起围观"千年奶酪"的故地。没人能相信它居然不见了。

人们开始为"千年奶酪"的遭遇想出各种各样疯狂的结论。有人说也许"千年奶酪"长出脚来，自己走掉。

我使出所有自制力才能抿着嘴巴。要不是罗利就站在旁边，老实说我不知道我能不能保持沉默。

　　那几个正在热烈争论"千年奶酪"到底怎么回事的家伙，就是昨天下午撺掇我和罗利打架的人。所以我知道，过不了多久，有人就会把两件事联系在一起，得出结论：我们一定对它做过什么。

　　罗利慌起来了。我也不怪他。如果"千年奶酪"消失的真相公之于世，罗利就完蛋了。他非得搬出我们这个州不可，甚至得搬出我们这个国家。

　　事到如今，我决定开口。

　　我跟大家说，我知道"千年奶酪"的情况。

　　我说，看到它粘在地上我就烦了，所以我决定将它彻底清理干净，一劳永逸。

　　有一秒钟的光景，大家都怔住了。

　　我以为他们会感谢我做了这么一件好事。结果，我大错特错。

　　我多希望自己能把故事稍微改头换面再讲出来。我清理掉了"千年奶酪"，想想这说明什么？就是说我被附体了！

六　月

<u>星期五</u>

　　呃，罗利有没有感激上星期我为他做的事我不知道，反正他没有说出口。 不过我们放学后又在一起玩了，所以我想这表明我和他的关系已经回复正常。

我可以坦白地说，到目前为止，沾上"奶酪附体"还不算太坏。

托它的福，体育课我就不用学集体舞了，因为没人愿意做我的拍档。我还可以每天独占整张桌子吃午饭。

今天是学年的最后一天。上完第八节课，学校给我们发了学年手册。

我马上翻到"班级之星"那一页，看到那张我期待已久的照片。

班级之星

罗利·杰弗逊

我只能说，谁要是想免费拿到一本学年手册，去餐厅后墙的垃圾箱里就可以刨出一本。

罗利得没得到"班级活宝"称号是他的事，我才不管。但要是他"死而复生"之后尾巴翘得太高，我会给他一个提醒：他可是那个吃了_____的人。

致　　谢

这本书的诞生有赖众多人士的协助，但我要特别感谢以下四位：

阿布拉姆斯出版集团的编辑查理·科赫曼，他对《小·屁孩日记》的大力支持远远超过我之前所希望的最大可能。 哪一个作家能让查理做自己的编辑都是幸运的。

杰斯·博拉里尔，他深知在线出版的力量和潜能，将格雷·赫夫利第一次带到大众面前。 我尤其感谢他的友谊和指导。

帕特里克，在帮助我完善这本书上他起了很大的作用。 当书里的某个笑话招人讨厌时，他总是勇敢地把这一点告诉我。

我的妻子，朱莉，没有她的鼎力支持，这本书不可能面世。

杰夫·金尼

作者简介

杰夫·金尼是一名网络游戏开发员和设计师。 他的童年在华盛顿特区度过。 1995 年他移居新英格兰州。 杰夫有两个儿子，威尔和格兰特。 他和妻儿现定居美国南部的马萨诸塞州。

TO MOM, DAD, RE, SCOTT, AND PATRICK

DIARY
of a
Wimpy Kid

②

by Jeff Kinney

DECEMBER

<u>Wednesday</u>

Well, if one good thing came out of the play, it's that I don't have to worry about the "Bubby" nickname anymore.

I saw Archie Kelly getting hassled in the hallway after fifth period today, so it looks like I can finally start to breathe a little easier.

<u>Sunday</u>

With all this stuff going on at school, I haven't even had time to think about Christmas. And it's less than ten days away.

In fact, the only thing that tipped me off that Christmas was coming was when Rodrick put his wish list up on the refrigerator.

Rodrick's Wish
List
_____

1. New drums
2. New van
3. Shrunken head

I usually make a big wish list every year, but this Christmas, all I really want is this video game called Twisted Wizard.

Tonight Manny was going through the Christmas catalog, picking out all the stuff he wants with a big red marker. Manny was circling every single toy in the catalog. He was even circling really expensive things like a giant motorized car and stuff like that.

So I decided to step in and give him some good big-brotherly advice.

I told him that if he circled stuff that was too expensive, he was going to end up with a bunch of clothes for Christmas. I said he should just pick three or four medium-priced gifts so he would end up with a couple of things he actually wanted.

But of course Manny just went back to circling everything again. So I guess he'll just have to learn the hard way.

When I was seven, the only thing I really wanted for Christmas was a Barbie Dream House. And NOT because I like girls' toys, like Rodrick said.

I just thought it would be a really awesome fort for my toy soldiers.

When Mom and Dad saw my wish list that year, they got in a big fight over it. Dad said there was no way he was getting me a dollhouse, but Mom said it was healthy for me to "experiment" with whatever kind of toys I wanted to play with.

Believe it or not, Dad actually won that argument. Dad told me to start my wish list over and pick some toys that were more "appropriate" for boys.

But I have a secret weapon when it comes to Christmas. My Uncle Charlie always gets me whatever I want. I told him I wanted the Barbie Dream House, and he said he'd hook me up.

On Christmas, when Uncle Charlie gave me my gift, it was NOT what I asked for. He must've walked into the toy store and picked up the first thing he saw that had the word "Barbie" on it.

So if you ever see a picture of me where I'm holding a Beach Fun Barbie, now at least you know the whole story.

Dad wasn't real happy when he saw what Uncle Charlie got me. He told me to either throw it out or give it away to charity.

But I kept it anyway. And OK, I admit maybe I took it out and played with it once or twice.

That's how I ended up in the emergency room two weeks later with a pink Barbie shoe stuck up my nose. And believe me, Rodrick has never let me hear the end of THAT.

<u>Thursday</u>
Tonight me and Mom went out to get a gift for the Giving Tree at church. The Giving Tree is basically a Secret Santa kind of thing where you get a gift for someone who is needy.

Mom picked out a red wool sweater for our Giving Tree guy.

I tried to talk Mom into getting something a lot cooler, like a TV or a slushie machine or something like that.

Because imagine if all you got on Christmas was
a wool sweater.

I'm sure our Giving Tree guy will throw his sweater
in the trash, along with the ten cans of yams we
sent his way during the Thanksgiving Food Drive.

Christmas

When I woke up this morning and went downstairs,
there were about a million gifts under the Christmas
tree. But when I started digging around, there
were hardly any gifts with my name on them.

But Manny made out like a bandit. He got EVERY single thing he circled in the catalog, no lie. So I'll bet he's glad he didn't listen to me.

I did find a couple things with my name on them, but they were mostly books and socks and stuff like that.

I opened my gifts in the corner behind the couch, because I don't like opening gifts near Dad. Whenever someone opens a gift, Dad swoops right in and cleans up after them.

I gave Manny a toy helicopter and I gave Rodrick a book about rock bands. Rodrick gave me a book, too, but of course he didn't wrap it. The book he got me was "Best of L'il Cutie." "L'il Cutie" is the worst comic in the newspaper, and Rodrick knows how much I hate it. I think this is the fourth year in a row I've gotten a "L'il Cutie" book from him.

I gave Mom and Dad their gifts. I get them the same kind of thing every year, but parents eat that stuff up.

The rest of the relatives started showing up around 11:00, and Uncle Charlie came at noon.

Uncle Charlie brought a big trash bag full of gifts, and he pulled my present out of the top of the bag.

The package was the exact right size and shape to be a Twisted Wizard game, so I knew Uncle Charlie came through for me. Mom got the camera ready and I tore open my gift.

But it was just an 8 x 10 picture of Uncle Charlie.

I guess I didn't do a good job of hiding my
disappointment, and Mom got mad. All I can say
is, I'm glad I'm still a kid, because if I had to
act happy about the kinds of gifts grown-ups
get, I don't think I could pull it off.

I went up to my room to take a break for a while. A couple minutes later, Dad knocked on my door. He told me he had my gift for me out in the garage, and the reason it was out there was because it was too big to wrap.

And when I walked down to the garage, there was a brand-new weight set.

100

That thing must have cost a fortune. I didn't have the heart to tell Dad that I kind of lost interest in the whole weight-lifting thing when the wrestling unit ended last week. So I just said "thanks" instead.

I think Dad was expecting me to drop down and start doing some reps or something, but I just excused myself and went back inside.

At about 6:00, all the relatives cleared out.

I was sitting on the couch watching Manny play with his toys, feeling pretty sorry for myself. Then Mom came up to me and said that she found a gift behind the piano with my name on it, and it said, "From Santa."

The box was way too big for Twisted Wizard, but Mom pulled the same "big box" trick on me last year when she got me a memory card for my video game system.

So I ripped open the package and pulled out my present. Only this wasn't Twisted Wizard, either. It was a giant red wool sweater.

At first I thought Mom was playing some kind of practical joke on me, because this sweater was the same kind we bought for our Giving Tree guy.

But Mom seemed pretty confused, too. She said she DID buy me a video game, and that she had no idea what the sweater was doing in my box.

And then I figured it out. I told Mom there must have been some kind of mix-up, and I got the Giving Tree guy's gift, and he got mine.

Mom said she used the same kind of wrapping paper for both of our gifts, so she must've written the wrong names on the tags.

But then Mom said that this was really a good thing, because the Giving Tree guy was probably really happy he got such a great gift.

I had to explain that you need a game system and a TV to play Twisted Wizard, so the game was totally useless to him.

Even though my Christmas was not going that great, I'm sure it was going a whole lot worse for the Giving Tree guy.

I kind of decided to throw in the towel* for this Christmas, and I headed up to Rowley's house.

I forgot to get a gift for Rowley, so I just slapped* a bow on the "L'il Cutie" book Rodrick gave me.

* slap
随便放上

And that seemed to do the trick.

Rowley's parents have a lot of money, so I can always count on them for a good gift.

But Rowley said that this year he picked out my gift himself. Then he brought me outside to show me what it was.

From the way Rowley was hyping* his present, I thought he must have gotten me a big-screen TV or a motorcycle or something.

* hype
大肆宣传

But once again, I let my hopes get too high.

Rowley got me a Big Wheel. I guess I would have thought this was a cool gift when I was in the third grade, but I have no idea what I'm supposed to do with one now.

Rowley was so enthusiastic about it that I tried my best to act like I was happy anyway.

We went back inside, and Rowley showed me his Christmas loot.

He sure got a lot more stuff than I did. He
even got Twisted Wizard, so at least I can play
it when I come up to his house. That is, until
Rowley's dad finds out how violent it is.

And boy, you have never seen someone as happy as
Rowley with his "L'il Cutie" book. His mom said it
was the only thing on his list that he didn't get.

Well, I'm glad SOMEONE got what they
wanted today.

New Year's Eve

In case you're wondering what I'm doing in my room at 9:00 p.m. on New Year's Eve, let me fill you in.

Earlier today, me and Manny were horsing around in the basement. I found a tiny black ball of thread on the carpet, and I told Manny it was a spider.

Then I held it over him pretending like I was going to make him eat it.

Right when I was about to let Manny go, he slapped my hand and made me drop the thread. And guess what? That fool swallowed it.

Well, Manny completely lost his mind. He ran
upstairs to where Mom was, and I knew I was
in big trouble.

Manny told Mom I made him eat a spider. I
told her there was no spider, and that it was
just a tiny ball of thread.

SNIFF

Mom brought Manny over to the kitchen table.
Then she put a seed, a raisin, and a grape on a
plate and told Manny to point to the thing
that was the closest in size to the piece of
thread he swallowed.

Manny took a while to look over the things on the plate.

Then he walked over to the refrigerator and pulled out an orange.

So that's why I got sent to bed at 7:00 and I'm not downstairs watching the New Year's Eve special on TV.

And that's also why my only New Year's resolution is to never play with Manny again.

110

JANUARY

<u>Wednesday</u>

I found a way to have some fun with the Big Wheel Rowley got me for Christmas. I came up with this game where one guy rides down the hill and the other guy tries to knock him off with a football.

Rowley was the first one down the hill, and I was the thrower.

It's a lot harder to hit a moving target than I thought. Plus, I didn't get a lot of practice. It took Rowley like ten minutes to walk the Big Wheel back up the hill after every trip down.

Rowley kept asking to switch places and have me be the one who rides the Big Wheel, but I'm no fool. That thing was hitting thirty-five miles an hour, and it didn't have any brakes.

Anyway, I never did knock Rowley off the Big Wheel today. But I guess I have something to work at over the rest of Christmas vacation.

Thursday
I was heading up to Rowley's today to play our Big Wheel game again, but Mom said I had to finish my Christmas thank-yous before I went out anywhere.

I thought I could just crank out my thank-you cards in a half hour, but when it came to actually writing them, my mind went blank.

Let me tell you, it's not easy writing thank-you notes for stuff you didn't want in the first place.

I started with the nonclothes items, because I thought they'd be easiest. But after two or three cards, I realized I was practically writing the same thing every time.

So I wrote up a general form on the computer with blanks for the things that needed to change. Writing the cards from there was a breeze.

Dear Aunt Lydia,

Thank you so much for the awesome encyclopedia !
How did you know I wanted that for Christmas?

I love the way the encyclopedia looks on my shelf !

All my friends will be so jealous that I have my very own encyclopedia .

Thank you for making this the best Christmas ever!

Sincerely, Greg

My system worked out pretty well for the first couple of gifts, but after that, not so much.

Dear Aunt Loretta,

Thank you so much for the awesome pants !
How did you know I wanted that for Christmas?

I love the way the pants looks on my legs !

All my friends will be so jealous that I have my very own pants .

Thank you for making this the best Christmas ever!

Sincerely, Greg

114

<u>Friday</u>
I finally knocked Rowley off the Big Wheel today, but it didn't happen the way I expected. I was trying to hit him in the shoulder, but I missed, and the football went under the front tire.

Rowley tried to break his fall by sticking out his arms, but he landed pretty hard on his left hand. I figured he'd just shake it off and get right back on the bike, but he didn't.

I tried to cheer him up, but all the jokes that usually crack him up weren't working.

So I knew he must be hurt pretty bad.

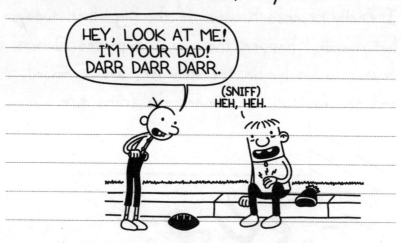

Monday

Christmas vacation is over, and now we're back at school. And you remember Rowley's Big Wheel accident? Well, he broke his hand, and now he has to wear a cast. And today, everyone was crowding around him like he was a hero or something.

I tried to cash in on some of Rowley's new popularity, but it totally backfired.

At lunch a bunch of girls invited Rowley over to their table so they could FEED him.

What really ticks me off about that is that Rowley is right-handed, and it's his LEFT hand that's broken. So he can feed himself just fine.

Tuesday

I realized Rowley's injury thing is a pretty good racket*, so I decided it was time for me to have an injury of my own.

* racket
幌子

I took some gauze from home, and I wrapped up my hand to make it look like it was hurt.

> IT'S A RAGING INFECTION CAUSED BY A SPLINTER THAT WAS LEFT UNTREATED!

I couldn't figure out why the girls weren't swarming me like they swarmed Rowley, but then I realized what the problem was.

See, the cast is a great gimmick because everyone wants to sign their name on it. But it's not exactly easy to sign gauze with a pen.

118

So I came up with a solution that I thought was just as good.

That idea was a total bust, too. My bandage did end up attracting attention from a couple of people, but believe me, they were not the type of people I was going for.

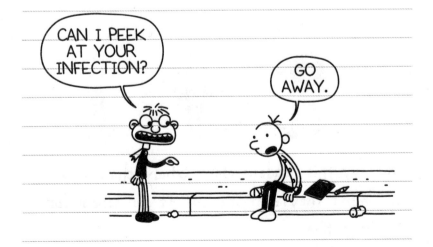

Monday

Last week we started the third quarter at school, so now I have a whole bunch of new classes. One of the classes I signed up for is something called Independent Study.

I WANTED to sign up for Home Economics 2, because I was pretty good at Home Ec 1.

But being good at sewing does not exactly buy you popularity points at school.

Anyway, this Independent Study thing is an experiment they're trying out at our school for the first time.

The idea is that the class gets assigned a project, and then you have to work on it together with no teacher in the room for the whole quarter.

The catch is that when you're done, everyone in your group gets the same grade. I found out that Ricky Fisher is in my class, which could be a big problem.

Ricky's big claim to fame is that he'll pick the gum off the bottom of a desk and chew it if you pay him fifty cents. So I don't really have high hopes for our final grade.

Tuesday
Today we got our Independent Study assignment, and guess what it is? We have to build a robot.

At first everybody kind of freaked out, because we thought we were going to have to build the robot from scratch.

121

But Mr. Darnell told us we don't have to build an actual robot. We just need to come up with ideas for what our robot might look like and what kinds of things it would be able to do.

Then he left the room, and we were on our own. We started brainstorming right away. I wrote down a bunch of ideas on the blackboard.

the robot would
do my homework
do the dishes
make my break-
                fast
brush my teeth

Everybody was pretty impressed with my ideas, but it was easy to come up with them. All I did was write down all the things I hate doing myself.

But a couple of the girls got up to the front of the room, and they had some ideas of their own. They erased my list and drew up their own plan.

They wanted to invent a robot that would give you dating advice and have ten types of lip gloss on its fingertips.

All us guys thought this was the stupidest idea we ever heard. So we ended up splitting into two groups, girls and boys. The boys went to the other side of the room while the girls stood around talking.

Now that we had all the serious workers in one place, we got to work. Someone had the idea that you can say your name to the robot and it can say it back to you.

HI BOB

Hi BOB it is very nice to meet you BOB.

But then someone else pointed out that you shouldn't be able to use bad words for your name, because the robot shouldn't be able to curse. So we decided we should come up with a list of all the bad words the robot shouldn't be able to say.

We came up with all the regular bad words, but then Ricky Fisher came up with twenty more the rest of us had never even heard before.

So Ricky ended up being one of the most valuable contributors on this project.

Right before the bell rang, Mr. Darnell came back in the room to check on our progress. He picked up the piece of paper we were writing on and read it over.

To make a long story short, Independent Study is canceled for the rest of the year.

Well, at least it is for us boys. So if the robots in the future are going around with cherry lip gloss for fingers, at least now you know how it all got started.

Thursday
In school today they had a general assembly and showed the movie "It's Great to Be Me," which they show us every year.

The movie is all about how you should be happy with who you are and not change anything about yourself.

To be honest with you, I think that's a really dumb message to be telling kids, especially the ones at my school.

Later on, they made an announcement that there are some openings on the Safety Patrols, and that got me thinking.

If someone picks on a Safety Patrol, it can get them suspended. The way I figure it, I can use any extra protection I can get.

Plus, I realized that maybe being in a position of authority could be good for me.

I went down to Mr. Winsky's office and signed myself up, and I got Rowley to sign up, too. I thought Mr. Winsky would make us do a bunch of chin-ups or jumping jacks or something to prove we were up for the job, but he just handed us our belts and badges on the spot.

Mr. Winsky said the openings were for a special assignment. Our school is right next to the elementary school, and they've got a half-day kindergarten there.

He wants us to walk the morning session kids home in the middle of the day. I realized that meant we would miss twenty minutes of Pre-Algebra. Rowley must have figured that out, too, because he started to speak up. But I gave him a wicked pinch underneath the desk before he could finish his sentence.

BUT WE WOULD MISS YAHOOEY!

I couldn't believe my luck. I was getting instant bully protection and a free pass from half of Pre-Algebra, and I didn't even have to lift a finger.

<u>Tuesday</u>
Today was our first day as Safety Patrols. Me and
Rowley don't technically have stations like all the
other Patrols, so that means we don't have to stand
out in the freezing cold for an hour before school.

But that didn't stop us from coming to the
cafeteria for the free hot chocolate they hand
out to the other Patrols before homeroom.

CLINK

Another great perk is that you get to show up
ten minutes late for first period.

HEL-LO!

I'm telling you, I've got it made with this Safety Patrol thing.

At 12:15, me and Rowley left school and walked the kindergartners home. The whole trip ate up forty-five minutes, and there were only twenty minutes of Pre-Algebra left when we got back.

Walking the kids home was no sweat. But one of the kindergartners started to smell a little funny, and I think maybe he had an accident in his pants.

He tried to let me know about it, but I just stared straight ahead and kept walking. I'll take these kids home, but believe me, I didn't sign up for any diaper duty.

<u>Wednesday</u>

Today it snowed for the first time this winter,
and school was canceled. We were supposed to
have a test in Pre-Algebra, and I've kind of
slacked off ever since I became a Safety Patrol.
So I was psyched.

I called Rowley and told him to come over. Me and
him have been talking about building the world's
biggest snowman for the past couple of years now.

And when I say the world's biggest snowman,
I'm not kidding. Our goal is to get into the
"Guinness Book of World Records."

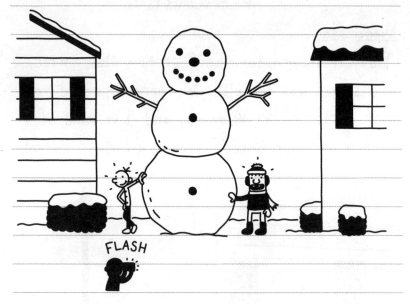

FLASH

But every time we've gotten serious about going
for the record, all the snow has melted, and
we've missed our window of opportunity. So this
year, I wanted to get started right away.

When Rowley came over, we started rolling the
first snowball to make the base. I figured the
base was going to have to be at least eight feet
tall on its own if we wanted to have a shot at
breaking the record. But the snowball got real
heavy, and we had to take a bunch of breaks in
between rolls so we could catch our breath.

During one of our breaks, Mom came outside to go
to the grocery store, but our snowball was blocking
her car in. So we got a little free labor out of her.

After our break, me and Rowley pushed that
snowball until we couldn't push it any farther.
But when we looked behind us, we saw the mess
we had made.

The snowball had gotten so heavy that it tore up all the sod Dad had just laid down this fall.

I was hoping it would snow a few more inches and cover up our tracks, but just like that, it stopped snowing.

Our plan to build the world's biggest snowman was starting to fall apart. So I came up with a better idea for our snowball.

Every time it snows, the kids from Whirley Street use our hill for sledding, even though this isn't their neighborhood.

So tomorrow morning, when the Whirley Street kids come marching up our hill, me and Rowley are going to teach those guys a lesson.

Thursday
When I woke up this morning, the snow was already starting to melt. So I told Rowley to hurry up and get down to my house.

While I was waiting for Rowley to show up, I watched Manny trying to build a snowman out of the piddly crumbs of snow that were left over from our snowball.

It was actually kind of pathetic.

I really couldn't help doing what I did next.
Unfortunately for me, right at that moment,
Dad was at the front window.

Dad was ALREADY mad at me for tearing up
the sod, so I knew I was in for it*. I heard the
garage door open and I saw Dad coming outside.
He marched right out carrying a snow shovel, and I
thought I was going to have to make a run for it.

* in for it
骑虎难下,
势必倒霉

But Dad was heading for my snowball, not me.
And in less than a minute, he reduced all our
hard work to nothing.

* get a kick
out of...
对……感到
极大乐趣

Rowley came by a few minutes later. I thought he might actually get a kick out of* what happened.

But I guess he had his heart set on rolling that snowball down the hill, and he was really mad. But get this: Rowley was mad at ME for what DAD did.

I told Rowley he was being a big baby, and we got in a shoving match. Right when it looked like we were going to get in an all-out fight, we got ambushed from the street.

It was a hit-and-run by the Whirley Street kids.

And if Mrs. Levine, my English teacher, was there, I'm sure she would have said the whole situation was "ironic."

Wednesday
Today at school they announced there's an opening for the cartoonist job in the school paper. There's only one comic slot, and up until now this kid named Bryan Little has been hogging it all to himself.

Bryan has this comic called "Wacky Dawg," and when it started off, it was actually pretty funny.

But lately, Bryan's been using his strip to handle his personal business. I guess that's why they gave him the axe.

As soon as I heard the news, I knew I had to try out. "Wacky Dawg" made Bryan Little a celebrity at our school, and I wanted to get in on some of that kind of fame.

I had a taste of what it's like to be famous at my school when I won honorable mention in this antismoking contest they had.

140

All I did was trace a picture from one of
Rodrick's heavy metal magazines, but luckily, no
one ever found out.

The kid who won first place is named Chris
Carney. And what kind of ticks me off* is that
Chris smokes at least a pack of cigarettes a day.

* tick...off
让……生气

Thursday
Me and Rowley decided to team up and do a
cartoon together. So after school today he came
over to my house, and we got to work.

We banged out a bunch of characters real
quick, but that turned out to be the easy
part. When we tried to think up some jokes,
we kind of hit a wall.

I finally came up with a good solution.

I made up a cartoon where the punch line of
every strip is "Zoo-Wee Mama!"

That way we wouldn't get bogged down with having
to write actual jokes, and we could concentrate on
the pictures.

142

For the first couple of strips, I did the writing and drew the characters, and Rowley drew the boxes around the pictures.

Rowley started complaining that he didn't have enough to do, so I let him write a few of the strips.

But to be honest with you, there was a pretty obvious drop in quality once Rowley started doing the writing.

Eventually I got kind of sick of the "Zoo-Wee Mama" idea and I pretty much let Rowley take over the whole operation.

And believe it or not, Rowley's drawing skills are worse than his writing skills.

I told Rowley maybe we should come up with some new ideas, but he just wanted to keep writing "Zoo-Wee Mamas." Then he packed up his comics and went home, which was fine by me. I don't really want to be partnered up with a kid who doesn't draw noses, anyway.

<u>Friday</u>

After Rowley left yesterday, I really got to work on some comics. I came up with this character called Creighton the Cretin, and I got on a roll.

CREIGHTON THE CRETIN   by Greg Heffley

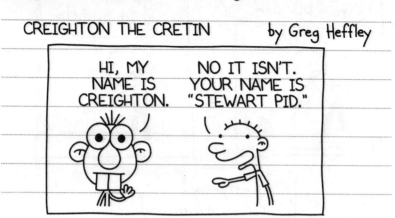

I must've banged out twenty strips, and I didn't even break a sweat.

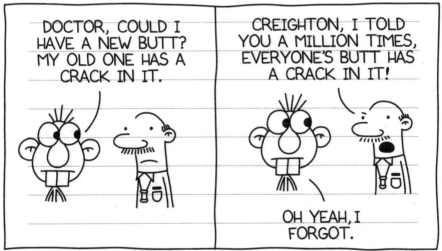

The great thing about these "Creighton the Cretin" comics is that with all the idiots running around my school, I will NEVER run out of new material.

When I got to school today, I took my comics to Mr. Ira's office. He's the teacher who runs the school newspaper.

But when I went to turn my strips in, I saw that there was a pile of comics from other kids who were trying out for the job.

Most of them were pretty bad, so I wasn't too worried about the competition.

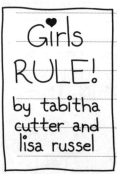

* darn
是damn的
委婉用法，
表诅咒

* shore
是sure的非
正式发音

One of the comics was called "Dumb Teachers,"
and it was written by this kid named Bill Tritt.

Bill is always in detention, so I guess he has a
bone to pick with just about every teacher in the
school, including Mr. Ira.

So I'm not too worried about the chances of
Bill's comic getting in, either.

There were actually one or two decent comics in
the bin. But I slipped them under a pile of
paperwork on Mr. Ira's desk.

Hopefully, those ones won't turn up until I'm in
high school.

<u>Thursday</u>
Today, during morning announcements, I got the news I was hoping for.

The paper came out today at lunch time, and everyone was reading it.

I really wanted to pick up a copy to see my name in print, but I decided to just play it cool for a while instead.

I sat at the end of the lunch table so there would be plenty of room for me to start signing autographs for my new fans. But nobody was coming over to tell me how great my comic was, and I started to get the feeling something was wrong.

I grabbed a paper and went into the bathroom to check it out. And when I saw my comic, I practically had a heart attack.

Mr. Ira told me he had made some "minor edits" to my comic. I thought he just meant he fixed spelling mistakes and stuff like that, but he totally butchered it.

The comic he ruined was one of my favorite ones, too. In the original, Creighton the Cretin is taking a math test, and he accidentally eats it. And then the teacher yells at him for being such a moron.

By the time Mr. Ira was done with it, you practically couldn't recognize it as the same strip.

Creighton the Curious Student   by Gregory Heffley

So I'm pretty sure I won't be signing autographs anytime soon.

Wednesday

Me and Rowley were enjoying our hot chocolate in the cafeteria with the rest of the Patrols today, and there was an announcement on the loudspeaker.

ROWLEY JEFFERSON, REPORT TO MR. WINSKY'S OFFICE IMMEDIATELY.

Rowley went down to Mr. Winsky's office, and when Rowley came back fifteen minutes later, he looked pretty shaken up.

Apparently Mr. Winsky got a call from a parent who said they witnessed Rowley "terrorizing" the kindergartners when he was supposed to be walking them home from school. And Mr. Winsky was really mad about it.

Rowley said Mr. Winsky yelled at him for about ten minutes and said his actions "disrespected the badge."

You know, I think I might just know what this is all about. Last week, Rowley had to take a quiz during fourth period, so I walked the kindergartners home on my own.

It had rained that morning, and there were a lot of worms on the sidewalk. So I decided to have some fun with the kids.

EEEEEEEE!!!

But some neighborhood lady saw what I was doing, and she yelled at me from her front porch.

It was Mrs. Irvine, who is friends with Rowley's mom. She must have thought I was Rowley, because I was borrowing his coat. And I wasn't about to correct her, either.

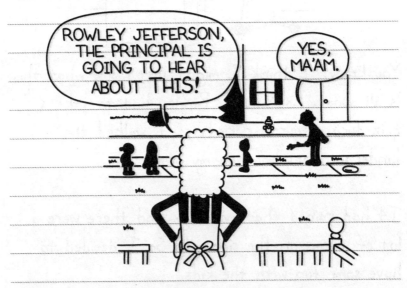

I forgot about the whole incident until today.

Anyway, Mr. Winsky told Rowley he's going to have to apologize to the kindergartners tomorrow morning, and that he's suspended from Patrols for a week.

I knew I should probably just tell Mr. Winsky it was me who chased the kids with the worms. But I wasn't ready to set the record straight just yet. I knew if I confessed, I'd lose my hot chocolate privileges. And that right there was enough to make me keep quiet for the time being.

At dinner tonight, Mom could tell something was bothering me, so she came up to my room afterward to talk.

I told her I was in a tough situation, and I didn't know what to do.

I got to give Mom credit for how she handled it. She didn't try to pry and get all the details. All she said was that I should try to do the "right thing," because it's our choices that make us who we are.

I figure that's pretty decent advice. But I'm still not 100% sure what I'm going to do tomorrow.

Thursday
Well, I was up all night tossing and turning over this Rowley situation, but I finally made up my mind. I decided the right thing to do was to just let Rowley take one for the team this time around.

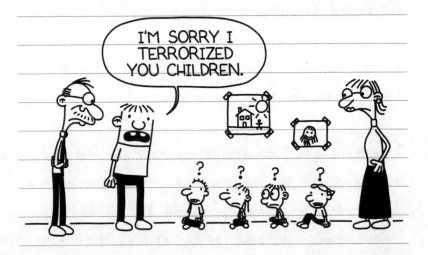

On the way home from school, I came clean with Rowley and told him the whole truth about what happened, and how it was me who chased the kids with the worms.

Then I told him there were lessons we could both learn from this. I told him I learned to be more careful about what I do in front of Mrs. Irvine's house, and that he learned a valuable lesson, too, which is this: Be careful about who you lend your coat to.

I GUESS THIS HAS BEEN A LEARNING EXPERIENCE FOR **BOTH** OF US!

To be honest with you, my message didn't seem to be getting through to Rowley.

We were supposed to hang out after school today, but he said he was just going to go home and take a nap.

I couldn't really blame him. Because if I didn't have my hot chocolate this morning, I wouldn't have had much energy, either.

When I got home, Mom was waiting for me at the front door.

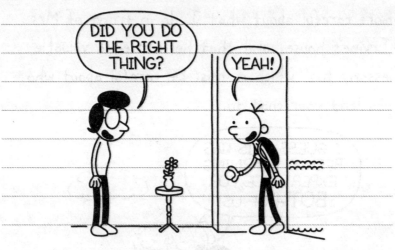

Mom took me out to get some ice cream as a special treat. And what this whole episode has taught me is that every once in a while, it's not such a bad idea to listen to your mother.

<u>Tuesday</u>

There was another announcement on the loudspeaker today, and to be honest with you, I kind of figured this one was coming.

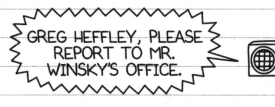

I knew it was just a matter of time before I got busted for what happened last week.

When I got to Mr. Winsky's office, he was really mad. Mr. Winsky told me that an "anonymous source" had informed him that I was the real culprit in the worm-chasing incident.

Then he told me I was relieved of my Safety Patrol duties "effective immediately."

Well, it doesn't take a detective to figure out that the anonymous source was Rowley.

I can't believe Rowley went and backstabbed me like that. While I was sitting there getting chewed out by Mr. Winsky, I was thinking, I need to remember to give my friend a lecture about loyalty.

Later on today, Rowley got reinstated as a Patrol. And get this: He actually got a PROMOTION. Mr. Winsky said Rowley had "exhibited dignity under false suspicion."

I thought about really letting Rowley have it for ratting me out like that, but then I realized something.

In June, all the officers in the Safety Patrols go on a trip to Six Flags, and they get to take along one friend. I need to make sure Rowley knows I'm his guy.

LET ME GET THIS FOR YOU, "CAPTAIN"!

Tuesday
Like I said before, the worst part of getting kicked off Safety Patrols is losing your hot chocolate privileges.

Every morning, I go to the back door of the cafeteria so Rowley can hook me up.

But either my friend has gone deaf or he's too busy kissing the other officers' butts to notice me at the window.

In fact, now that I think of it, Rowley has been TOTALLY giving me the cold shoulder lately. And that's really lame, because if I recall correctly, HE'S the one that sold ME out.

Even though Rowley has been a total jerk lately, I tried to break the ice with him today, anyway. But even THAT didn't seem to work.

APRIL

Friday

Ever since the worm incident, Rowley has been
hanging out with Collin Lee every day after school.
What really stinks is that Collin is supposed to
be MY backup friend.

Those guys are acting totally ridiculous. Today,
Rowley and Collin were wearing these matching
T-shirts, and it made me just about want to vomit.

After dinner tonight, I saw Rowley and Collin
walking up the hill together, chumming it up*.

* chum up
结为好友

Collin had his overnight bag, so I knew they were going to do a sleepover at Rowley's.

And I thought, Well, two can play at THAT game. The best way to get back at Rowley was to get a new best friend of my own. But unfortunately, the only person who came to mind right at that moment was Fregley.

I went up to Fregley's with my overnight bag so Rowley could see I had other friend options, too.

When I got there, Fregley was in his front yard stabbing a kite with a stick. That's when I started to think maybe this wasn't the best idea after all.

PANT
PANT
PANT

But Rowley was in his front yard, and he was watching me. So I knew there was no turning back.

I invited myself into Fregley's house. His mom said she was excited to see Fregley with a "playmate," which was a term I was not too enthusiastic about.

Me and Fregley went upstairs to his room. Fregley tried to get me to play Twister with him, so I made sure I stayed ten feet away from him at all times.

I decided that I should just pull the plug* on this stupid idea and go home. But every time I looked out the window, Rowley and Collin were still in Rowley's front yard.

* pull the plug
退出，停止

I didn't want to leave until those guys went back inside. But things started to get out of hand with Fregley pretty quickly. When I was looking out the window, Fregley broke into my backpack and ate the whole bag of jelly beans I had in there.

Fregley's one of these kids who's not supposed to eat any sugar, so two minutes later, he was bouncing off the walls.

Fregley started acting like a total maniac, and he chased me all around his upstairs.

I kept thinking he was going to come down off of his sugar high, but he didn't. Eventually, I locked myself in his bathroom to wait him out.

Around 11:30, it got quiet out in the hallway. That's when Fregley slipped a piece of paper under the door.

I picked it up and read it.

Dear Gregory,

I'm very sorry I chased you with a booger* on my finger. Here, I put it on this paper so you can get me back.

* booger
鼻屎

That's the last thing I remember before I
blacked out*.

* black out
丧失意识,
昏倒

I came to my senses a few hours later. After I
woke up, I cracked the door open, and I heard
snoring coming from Fregley's room. So I decided
to make a run for it.

Mom and Dad were not happy with me for getting
them out of bed at 2:00 in the morning. But by
that point, I could really care less.

<u>Monday</u>

Well, me and Rowley have officially been ex-friends for about a month now, and to be honest with you, I'm better off without him.

I'm glad I can just do whatever I want without having to worry about carrying all that dead weight around.

Lately I've been hanging out in Rodrick's room after school and going through his stuff. The other day, I found one of his middle school yearbooks.

Rodrick wrote on everybody's picture in his yearbook, so you can tell how he felt about all the kids in his grade.

Every once in a while, I see Rodrick's old classmates around town. And I have to remember to thank Rodrick for making church a lot more interesting.

But the page in Rodrick's yearbook that's really interesting is the Class Favorites page.

That's where they put pictures of the kids who get voted Most Popular and Most Talented and all that.

Rodrick wrote on his Class Favorites page, too.

MOST LIKELY TO SUCCEED

Bill Watson   Kathy Nguyen

You know, this Class Favorites thing has really got my gears turning.

If you can get yourself voted onto the Class Favorites page, you're practically an immortal. Even if you don't live up to what you got picked for, it doesn't really matter, because it's on permanent record.

People still treat Bill Watson like he's something special, even though he ended up dropping out of high school.

We still run into him at the Food Barn every once in a while.

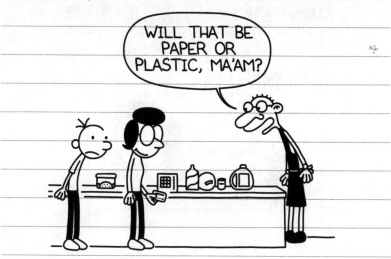

So here's what I'm thinking: This school year has been kind of a bust, but if I can get voted as a Class Favorite, I'll go out on a high note.

I've been trying to think of a category I have a shot at. Most Popular and Most Athletic are definitely out, so I'm going to have to find something that's a little bit more in reach.

At first I thought maybe I should wear really nice clothes for the rest of the year so I can get Best Dressed.

But that would mean I would have to get my picture taken with Jenna Stewart, and she dresses like a Pilgrim.

Wednesday

Last night I was lying in bed, and it hit me: I should go for Class Clown.

It's not like I'm known for being real funny at school or anything, but if I can pull off one big prank right before voting, that could do it.

YEEOWW!

THUMB
TACK

MAY

Thursday

Today I was trying to figure out how I was going to sneak a thumbtack onto Mr. Worth's chair in History when he said something that made me rethink my plan.

Mr. Worth told us he has a dentist's appointment tomorrow, so we're going to have a substitute. Subs are like comic gold. You can say just about anything you want, and you can't get in trouble.

GREG HEFFLEY, WILL YOU PLEASE DO THIS PROBLEM?

EXCUSE ME?

WELL, I HARDLY THINK THAT'S...

YOUR MAMA!

YOUR BIG FANNY GRANNY!

YOUR SLAP-HAPPY GRANDPAPPY!

<u>Friday</u>
I walked into my History class today, ready
to execute my plan. But when I got to the
door, guess who the substitute teacher was?

Of all the people in the world to be our sub
today, it was Mom. I thought Mom's days of
getting involved at my school were over.

She used to be one of those parents who came
in to help out in the classroom. But that all
changed after Mom volunteered to be a
chaperone for our field trip to the zoo when
I was in third grade.

Mom had prepared all sorts of material to help us kids appreciate the different exhibits, but all anyone wanted to do was watch the animals go to the bathroom.

Anyway, Mom totally foiled my plan to win Class Clown. I'm just lucky there's not a category called Biggest Mama's Boy, because after today, I'd win that one in a landslide*.

* landslide
压倒性的胜
利

<u>Wednesday</u>

The school paper came out again today. I quit my job as school cartoonist after "Creighton the Curious Student" came out, and I didn't really care who they picked to replace me.

But everyone was laughing at the comics page at lunch, so I picked up a copy to see what was so funny. And when I opened it up, I couldn't believe my eyes.

It was "Zoo-Wee Mama." And of course Mr. Ira didn't change a single WORD of Rowley's strip.

Zoo-Wee Mama   by Rowley Jefferson

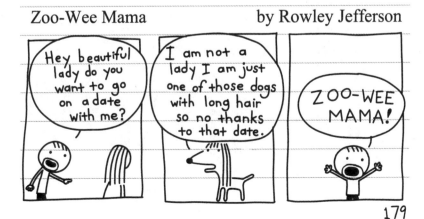

So now Rowley's getting all the fame that was supposed to be mine.

Even the teachers are kissing Rowley's butt*. I almost lost my lunch when Mr. Worth dropped his chalk in History class—

<u>Monday</u>

This "Zoo-Wee Mama" thing has really got me worked up. Rowley is getting all the credit for a comic that we came up with together. I figured the least he could do was put my name on the strip as the co-creator.

So I went up to Rowley after school and told him that's what he was gonna have to do. But Rowley said "Zoo-Wee Mama" was all HIS idea and that I didn't have anything to do with it.

I guess we must've been talking pretty loud, because the next thing you knew, we attracted a crowd.

The kids at my school are ALWAYS itching to see a fight. Me and Rowley tried to walk away, but those guys weren't going to let us go until they saw us throw some punches.

I've never been in a real fight before, so I didn't know how I was supposed to stand or hold my fists or anything. And you could tell Rowley didn't know what he was doing either, because he just started prancing around like a leprechaun.

I was pretty sure I could take Rowley in a fight, but the thing that made me nervous was the fact that Rowley takes karate. I don't know what kind of hocus-pocus they teach in Rowley's karate classes, but the last thing I needed was for him to lay me out right there on the blacktop.

Before me or Rowley made a move, there was a screeching sound in the school parking lot. A bunch of teenagers had stopped their pickup truck, and they started piling out.

I was just happy that everyone's attention was on the teenagers instead of me and Rowley. But all the other kids took off when the teenagers started heading our way.

And then I realized that these teenagers looked awfully familiar.

That's when it hit me. These were the same guys who chased me and Rowley around on Halloween night, and they had finally caught up with us.

But before we could make a run for it, we had our
arms pinned behind our backs.

Those guys wanted to teach us a lesson for
taunting them on Halloween night, and they
started arguing over what they should do with us.

But to be honest with you, I was more concerned
about something else. The Cheese was only a few
feet from where we were standing on the blacktop,
and it was looking nastier than ever.

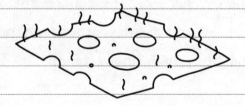

The big teenager must have caught my eye,
because the next thing I knew, he was looking
at the Cheese, too. And I guess that gave him
the idea he was looking for.

Rowley got singled out first. The big kid grabbed
Rowley and dragged him over to the Cheese.

Now, I don't want to say exactly what happened
next. Because if Rowley ever tries to run for
President and someone finds out what these guys
made him do, he won't have a chance.

So I'll put it to you this way: They made Rowley
_____ the Cheese.

I knew they were gonna make me do it, too. I started to panic, because I knew I wasn't going to be able to fight my way out of this situation.

* fast talk
花言巧语

So I did some fast talking* instead.

And believe it or not, it actually worked.

I guess the teenagers were satisfied they had made their point, because after they made Rowley finish off the rest of the Cheese, they let us go. They got back in their truck and took off down the road.

Me and Rowley walked home together. But neither one of us really said anything on the way back.

I thought about mentioning to Rowley that maybe he could have pulled out a couple of his karate moves back there, but something told me to hold off on that thought for right now.

SHUDDER
SHUDDER

<u>Tuesday</u>
At school today, the teachers let us outside
after lunch.

It took about five seconds for someone to
realize the Cheese was missing from its spot on
the blacktop.

Everybody crowded around to look at where the
Cheese used to be. Nobody could believe it was
actually gone.

People started coming up with these crazy theories
about what happened to it. Somebody said that
maybe the Cheese grew legs and walked away.

It took all my self-control to keep my mouth shut. And if Rowley wasn't standing right there, I honestly don't know if I could have kept quiet.

A couple of the guys who were arguing over what happened to the Cheese were the same ones who were egging me and Rowley on* yesterday afternoon. So I knew it wasn't going to be long before someone put two and two together and figured out that we must have had something to do with it.

* egg...on
鼓动，怂勇

Rowley was starting to panic, and I don't blame him, either. If the truth ever came out about how the Cheese disappeared, Rowley would be finished. He'd have to move out of the state, and maybe even the country.

That's when I decided to speak up.

I told everyone that I knew what happened to the Cheese. I said I was sick of it being on the blacktop, and I just decided to get rid of it once and for all.

For a second there, everyone just froze. I thought people were going to start thanking me for what I did, but boy, was I wrong.

I really wish I had worded my story a little differently. Because if I threw away the Cheese, guess what that meant? It meant that I have the Cheese Touch.

JUNE

<u>Friday</u>

Well, if Rowley appreciated what I did for him last week, he hasn't said it. But we've started hanging out after school again, so I guess that means me and him are back to normal.

I can honestly say that so far, having the Cheese Touch hasn't been all that bad.

It got me out of doing the Square Dance unit in Phys Ed, because no one would partner up with me. And I've had the whole lunch table to myself every day.

Today was the last day of school, and they handed out yearbooks after eighth period.

I flipped to the Class Favorites page, and here's the picture that was waiting for me.

CLASS CLOWN

Rowley Jefferson

All I can say is, if anyone wants a free yearbook, they can dig one out of the trash can in the back of the cafeteria.

You know, Rowley can have Class Clown for all I care. But if he ever gets too big for his britches*, I'll just remind him that he was the guy who ate the _____.

*too big
for one's
britches
自高自大,
摆架子

192

ACKNOWLEDGMENTS

There are many people who helped bring this book to life, but four individuals deserve special thanks:

Abrams editor Charlie Kochman, whose advocacy for *Diary of a Wimpy Kid* has been beyond what I could have hoped for. Any writer would be lucky to have Charlie as an editor.

Jess Brallier, who understands the power and potential of online publishing, and helped Greg Heffley reach the masses for the first time. Thanks especially for your friendship and mentorship.

Patrick, who was instrumental in helping me improve this book, and who wasn't afraid to tell me when a joke stunk.

My wife, Julie, without whose incredible support this book would not have become a reality.

ABOUT THE AUTHOR

Jeff Kinney is an online game developer and designer. He spent his childhood in the Washington D.C. area and moved to New England in 1995. Jeff lives in southern Massachusetts with his wife, Julie, and their two sons, Will and Grant.

望子快乐

朱子庆

　　在一个人的一生中，"与有荣焉"的机会或有，但肯定不多。因为儿子译了一部畅销书，而老爸被邀涂鸦几句，像这样的与荣，我想，即使放眼天下，也没有几人领得吧。

　　儿子接活儿翻译《小屁孩日记》时，还在读着大三。这是安安第一次领译书稿，多少有点紧张和兴奋吧，起初他每译几段，便飞鸽传书，不一会儿人也跟过来，在我面前"项庄舞剑"地问："有意思么？有意思么？"怎么当时我就没有作乐不可支状呢？于今想来，我竟很有些后悔。对于一个喂饱段子与小品的中国人，若说还有什么洋幽默能令我们"绝倒"，难！不过，当安安译成杀青之时，图文并茂，我得以从头到尾再读一遍，我得说，这部书岂止有意思呢，读了它使我有一种冲动，假如时间可以倒流，我很想尝试重新做一回父亲！我不免窃想，安安在译它的时候，不知会怎样腹诽我这个老爸呢！

　　我宁愿儿子是书里那个小屁孩！

　　你可能会说，你别是在做秀吧，小屁孩格雷将来能出息成个什么样子，实在还很难说……这个质疑，典型地出诸一个中国人之口，出之于为父母的中国人之口。望子成龙，一定要孩子出息成个什么样子，虽说初衷也是为了孩子，但最终却是苦了孩子。"生年不满百，常怀千岁忧。"现在，由于这深重的忧患，我们已经把成功学启示的模式都做到胎教了！而望子快乐，有谁想过？从小就快乐，快乐一生？惭愧，我也是看了《小屁孩日记》才想到这点，然而儿子已不再年少！我觉得很有些对不住儿子！

我从来没有对安安的"少年老成"感到过有什么不妥，毕竟少年老成使人放心。而今读其译作而被触动，此心才为之不安起来。我在想，比起美国的小屁孩格雷和他的同学们，我们中国的小屁孩们是不是活得不很小屁孩？是不是普遍地过于负重、乏乐和少年老成？而当他们将来长大，娶妻（嫁夫）生子（女），为人父母，会不会还要循此逻辑再造下一代？想想安安少年时，起早贪黑地读书、写作业，小四眼，十足一个书呆子，类似格雷那样的调皮、贪玩、小有恶搞、缰绳牢笼不住地敢于尝试和行动主义……太缺少了。印象中，安安最突出的一次，也就是读小学三年级时，做了一回带头大哥，拔了校园里所有单车的气门芯并四处派发，仅此而已吧（此处，请在家长指导下阅读）。

说点别的吧。中国作家写的儿童文学作品，很少能引发成年读者的阅读兴趣。安徒生童话之所以风靡天下，在于它征服了成年读者。在我看来，《小屁孩日记》也属于成人少年兼宜的读物，可以父子同修！谁没有年少轻狂？谁没有豆蔻年华？只不过呢，对于为父母者，阅读它，会使你由会心一笑而再笑，继以感慨系之，进而不免有所自省，对照和检讨一下自己和孩子的关系，以及在某些类似事情的处理上，自己是否欠妥？等等。它虽系成人所作，书中对孩子心性的把握，却准确传神；虽非心理学著作，对了解孩子的心理和行为，也不无参悟和启示。品学兼优和顽劣不学的孩子毕竟是少数，小屁孩格雷是"中间人物"的一个玲珑典型，着实招人怜爱——在格雷身上，有着我们彼此都难免有的各样小心思、小算计、小毛病，就好像阿Q，读来透着与我们有那么一种割不断的血缘关系，这，也许就是此书在美国乃至全球都特别畅销的原因吧！

最后我想申明的是，第一读者身份在我是弥足珍惜的，因为，宝贝儿子出生时，第一眼看见他的是医生，老爸都摊不上第一读者呢！

我眼中的 ……

好书，爱不释手！

★ 读者 王汐子（女，2009年留学美国，攻读大学传媒专业）《小屁孩日记》在美国掀起的阅读风潮可不是盖的，在我留学美国的这一年中，不止一次目睹这套书对太平洋彼岸人民的巨大影响。高速公路上巨大的广告宣传牌就不用说了，我甚至在学校书店买课本时看到了这套书被大大咧咧地摆上书架，"小屁孩"的搞笑日记就这样理直气壮地充当起了美国大学生的课本教材！为什么这套书如此受欢迎？为什么一个普普通通的小男孩能让这么多成年人捧腹大笑？也许可以套用一个万能句式"每个人心中都有一个XXX"。每个人心中都有一个小屁孩，每个人小时候也有过这样的时光，每天都有点鸡毛蒜皮的小烦恼，像作业这么多怎么办啦，要考试了书都没有看怎么办啦……但是大部分时候还是因为调皮捣乱被妈妈教训……就这样迷迷糊糊地走过了"小屁孩"时光，等长大后和朋友们讨论后才恍然大悟，随即不禁感慨，原来那时候我们都一样呀……是呀，全世界的小屁孩都一样！

★ 读者 zhizhimother（发表于2009-06-12）在杂志上看到这书的介绍，一时冲动在当当上下了单，没想到，一买回来一家人抢着看，笑得前仰后合。我跟女儿一人抢到一本，老公很不满意，他嘟囔着下一本出的时候他要第一个看。看多了面孔雷同的好孩子的书，看到这本，真是深有感触，我们的孩子其实都是这样长大的～～

轻松阅读　捧腹大笑

★　这是著名的畅销书作家小巫的儿子Sam口述的英语和中文读后感：I like *Diary* of a *Wimpy Kid* because Greg is an average child just like us. His words are really funny and the illustrations are hilarious. His stories are eventful and most of them involve silliness.

我喜欢《小屁孩日记》，因为Greg是跟我们一样的普通孩子。他的故事很好玩儿，令我捧腹大笑，他做的事情很搞笑，有点儿傻呼呼的。书里的插图也很幽默。

★　读者 dearm暖baby（发表于2009-07-29）我12岁了，过生日时妈妈给我买了这样两本书，真的很有趣！一半是中文，一半是英文，彻底打破了"英文看不懂看下面中文"的局限！而且这本书彻底地给我来了次大放松，"重点中学"的压力也一扫而光！总之，两个字：超赞！

★　读者 mei298（发表于2010-01-23）儿子超喜欢，边看边大笑。买了1~4册，没几天就看完了，特别喜欢那一段"弗雷格跟我在同一个班上体育课，他的语言自成一家，比如说他要去厕所的时候，他就说——果汁！果汁！！！我们已经大致清楚弗雷格那套了，不过我看老师们大概还没弄懂。老师说——好吧，小伙子……你可真难侍候！还端来了一杯汽水。"为了这段话，儿子笑了一整天，到睡觉的时候想想还笑。

孩子爱上写日记了！

★ 读者 ddian2003（发表于2009-12-22）正是于丹的那几句话吸引我买下了这套书。自己倒没看，但女儿却用了三天学校的课余时间就看完了，随后她大受启发，连着几天都写了日记。现在这书暂时搁在书柜里，已和女儿约定，等她学了英文后再来看一遍，当然要看书里的英文了。所以这书还是买得物有所值的。毕竟女儿喜欢！！

做个"不听话的好孩子"

★ 读者 水真爽（发表于2010-03-27）这套书是买给我上小学二年级的儿子的。有时候他因为到该读书的时间而被要求从网游下来很恼火。尽管带着气，甚至眼泪，可是读起这本书来，总是能被书中小屁孩的种种淘气出格行为和想法弄得哈哈大笑。书中的卡通漫画也非常不错。这种文字漫画形式的日记非常具有趣味性，老少咸宜。对低年级孩子或爱画漫画的孩子尤其有启发作用。更重要的是提醒家长们好好留意观察这些"不怎么听话"的小屁孩们的内心世界，他们的健康成长需要成人的呵护引导，但千万不要把他们都变成只会"听大人话"的好孩子。

★ 读者 寂寞朱丽叶（发表于2009-06-10）最近我身边的朋友都在看这本书，出于好奇我也买了一套，美国"囧男孩"格雷满脑子的鬼主意，虽然不是人们心目中好孩子的形象，但很真实，我很喜欢他，还有点羡慕他，我怎么没有他有趣呢。

对照《小屁孩日记》分享育儿体验

★ 读者 gjrzj2002@＊＊＊.＊＊＊（发表于2010-05-21）看完四册书，我想着自己虽然不可能有三个孩子，但一个孩子的成长经历至今仍记忆犹新。儿子还是幼儿的时候，比较像曼尼，在爸妈眼中少有缺点，真是让人越看越爱，想要什么就基本上能得到什么。整个幼儿期父母对孩子肯定大过否定。上了小学，儿子的境地就不怎么从容了，上学的压力时时处处在影响着他，小家伙要承受各方面的压力，父母、老师、同学，太过我行我素、大而化之都是行不通的，比如没写作业的话，老师、家长的批评和提醒是少不了的，孩子在慢慢学着适应这种生活，烦恼也随之而来，这一阶段比较像格雷，虽然儿子的思维还没那么丰富，快乐和烦恼的花样都没那么多，但处境差不多，表扬和赞美不像以前那样轻易就能得到了。儿子青年时代会是什么样子我还不得而知，也不可想象，那种水到渠成的阶段要靠前面的积累，我希望自己到时候能平心静气，坦然接受，无论儿子成长成什么样子。

气味相投的好伙伴

★ 上海市外国语大学附属第一实验中学，中预10班，沈昕仪Elaine：《小屁孩日记》读来十分轻松。虽然没有用十分华丽的语言，却使我感受到了小屁孩那缤纷多彩的生活，给我带来无限的欢乐。那精彩的插图、幽默的文字实在是太有趣了，当中的故事在我们身边都有可能发生，让人身临其境。格雷总能说出我的心里话，他是和我有着共同语言的朋友。所以他们搞的恶作剧一直让我跃跃欲试，也想找一次机会尝试一下。不知别的读者怎么想，我觉得格雷挺喜欢出风头的。我也是这样的人，总怕别人无视了自己。当看到格雷蹦出那些稀奇古怪的点子的时候，我多想帮他一把啊——毕竟我们是"气味相投"的同类人嘛。另一方面，我身处在外语学校，时刻都需要积累英语单词，但这件事总是让我觉得枯燥乏味。而《小屁孩日记》帮了我的大忙：我在享受快乐阅读的同时，还可以对照中英文学到很多常用英语单词。我发现其实生活中还有很多事情值得我们去用笔写下来。即使是小事，这些童年的故事也是很值得我们回忆的。既然还生活在童年，还能够写下那些故事，又何乐而不为呢？

画出我心中的"小屁孩"

邓博笔下的赫夫利一家

读者@童_Cc.@曲奇做的"小屁孩"手抄报

亲爱的读者，你看完这本书后，有什么感想吗？请来电话或是登录本书的博客与我们分享吧！等本书再版时，这里也许换上了你的读后感呢！

　　我们的电话号码是：020-83795744，博客地址是：blog.sina.com.cn/wimpykid，微博地址是：weibo.com/wimpywimpy。

悦读 "小·屁孩"

《小·屁孩日记①——鬼屋创意》

在日记里，格雷记叙了他如何驾驭充满冒险的中学生活，如何巧妙逃脱学校歌唱比赛，最重要的是如何不让任何人发现他的秘密。他经常想捉弄人反被人捉弄；他常常想做好事却弄巧成拙；他屡屡身陷尴尬境遇竟逢 "凶" 化吉。他不是好孩子，也不是坏孩子，就只是普通的孩子；他有点自私，但重要关头也会挺身而出保护朋友……

《小·屁孩日记②——谁动了千年奶酪》

在《小屁孩日记②》里，主人公格雷度过一个没有任何奇迹发生的圣诞节。为打发漫长无聊的下雪天，他和死党罗利雄心勃勃地想要堆出 "世界上最大的雪人"，却因为惹怒老爸，雪人被销毁；格雷可是不甘寂寞的，没几天，他又找到乐子了，在送幼儿园小朋友过街的时候，他制造了一起 "虫子事件" 吓唬小朋友，并嫁祸罗利，从而导致一场 "严重" 的友情危机……格雷能顺利化解危机，重新赢得好朋友罗利的信任吗？

《小·屁孩日记③——好孩子不撒谎》

在本册里，格雷开始了他的暑假生活。慢着，别以为他的假期会轻松愉快。其实他整个暑

假都被游泳训练班给毁了。他还自作聪明地导演了一出把同学齐拉格当成隐形人的闹剧，他以为神不知鬼不觉就可以每天偷吃姜饼，终于在圣诞前夜东窗事发，付出了巨大的代价……

《小·屁孩日记④——偷鸡不成蚀把米》

本集里，格雷仿佛落入了他哥哥罗德里克的魔掌中一般，怎么也逃脱不了厄运：他在老妈的威逼利诱下跟罗德里克学爵士鼓，却只能在一旁干看罗德里克自娱自乐；与好友罗利一起偷看罗德里克窝藏的鬼片，却不幸玩过火害罗利受伤，为此格雷不得不付出惨重代价——代替罗利在全校晚会上表演魔术——而他的全部表演内容就是为一个一年级小朋友递魔术道具。更大的悲剧还在后面，他不惜花"重金"购买罗德里克的旧作业想要蒙混过关，却不幸买到一份不及格的作业。最后，他暑假误入女厕所的囧事还被罗德里克在全校大肆宣扬……格雷还有脸在学校混吗？他的日记还能继续下去吗？

《小·屁孩日记⑤——午餐零食大盗》

格雷在新的一年里展开了他的学校生活：克雷格老师的词典不翼而飞，于是每天课间休息时所有同学都被禁止外出，直至字典被找到；格雷的午餐零食从糖果变成了两个水果，他怀疑是哥哥罗德里克偷了零食，誓要查出真相。因为午餐零食闹的"糖荒"，让格雷精神不振，总是在下午的课堂上打瞌睡。格雷没有多余的零用钱，不能自己买糖果，于是他想到了自己埋下的时光宝盒——里面放着三美元的钞票。格雷挖出时光宝盒，暂时缓解了"糖荒"。另一边厢，学校即将举行第一次的情人节舞会。格雷对漂亮的同班同学荷莉心仪已久，就决定趁舞会好好表现。在舞会上，他成功与荷莉互相交换了情人节卡片，并想邀请荷莉跳舞，于是他向人群中的荷莉走去……

《小·屁孩日记⑥——可怕的炮兵学校》

格雷想尽一切办法让老爸摆脱一些可怕的念头。格雷的老爸一直希望他能加强锻炼，就让他加入了周末的足球队。格雷在足球队吃尽了苦头：他先被教练派去当球童，在荆棘丛里捡球累了个半死；然后又被要求坐在寒风中观赛，冷得他直打哆嗦；后来他自以为聪明地选择了后备守门员的位置，最后却因为正选守门员受伤而不得不披挂上阵。在输掉足球比赛后，格雷觉得老爸因此而生气了。未想老爸又冒出另一个更可怕的念头：把格雷送进炮兵学校。格雷却自动请缨加入周末的童子军，因为这样一来他就不必再去参加足球训练了。然而，在童子军的父子营中，格雷又为老爸惹来麻烦……老爸决定在这个学期结束后，就立刻把格雷送进炮兵学校。眼看暑假就要开始了，格雷因此坐立不安……

《小·屁孩日记⑦——从天而降的巨债》

暑假刚开始，格雷就与老爸老妈展开了拉锯战：老爸老妈坚持认为孩子放暑假就应该到户外去活动，但格雷却宁愿躲在家里打游戏机、看肥皂剧。不得已之下，格雷跟着死党罗利到乡村俱乐部玩，两人在那儿吃了一点东西，就欠下了83美元的"巨债"。于是，他们不得不想尽一切办法打工还债……

他们能把债务还清吗？格雷又惹出了什么笑话？

《小·屁孩日记⑧——"头盖骨摇晃机"的幸存者》

老妈带全家上了旅行车，看到防晒霜和泳
衣，格雷满心以为是去海滩度假，却原来只是去
水上乐园——一个令格雷吃过很多苦头的地方，
过去的不愉快记忆也就罢了，这次好不容易做好
一切准备，广播却通知"因闪电天气停止营
业"；回到家里又怎样呢？格雷发现他心爱的鱼
惨遭罗德里克宠物鱼的"毒口"；盼望已久的小狗阿甜来了，非但不
是补偿，反而使格雷的生活一团糟；格雷发现救生员是希尔斯小姐，
这使得他一改对于小镇游泳场的糟糕看法，小心眼儿活动起来；妈妈
安排了一个格雷与爸爸改善关系的机会，可是格雷却用"甲壳虫小
姐"召来了警察，搞得老爸灰溜溜的，他们关系更僵；老妈处心积虑
安排格雷和死党罗利的一家去了海滩，格雷却又惹了祸……

我们可爱又倒霉的格雷啊，他该如何处理这一切？"头盖骨摇
晃机"又是怎么回事？

《小·屁孩日记⑨——老妈不在家》

格雷的老妈在家庭会议中宣布自己要重返校园进修，这个消息让格雷父子措手不及：这意味着父子四人要自己做晚饭，还要分摊原来由老妈包揽的家务活……于是，他们开始了"灾民"般的生活。另一边厢，学校在新学期开了健康教育课，据说会讲一些老师从前避而不谈的内容；这门课煞有介事地要求家长签同意书，又让男生女生分班上课，这让格雷对课程的内容充满期待。

老妈不在家，格雷会在家里闹翻天吗？格雷在健康教育课上究竟能听到些什么内容？

《小·屁孩日记⑩——"屁股照片"风波》

小屁孩格雷在本集中，参加了学校组织的"关门"派对，在分组拍照游戏竞赛中，为了让其他组成员猜不出他们组拍的是谁而取得游戏的奖励，格雷和伙伴们想了各种办法，终于拍出了一幅大家都比较满意的照片，可是，老师认为他们的这幅照片拍的是人体某个部位，格调非常不雅……这让格雷和伙伴们觉得冤透了。事情最后落得什么样的结果呢？